In Search
of
Christian Leadership
Qualities and Role

Volume II

In Search
of
Christian Leadership
Qualities and Role

Volume II

John Zechariah

2015

In Search of Christian Leadership: Qualities and Role - Volume II —
jointly published by the Rev. Dr. Ashish Amos of the Indian Society for
Promoting Christian Knowledge (ISPCK), Post Box 1585, Kashmere Gate,
Delhi-110006 and Asian Academy for Leadership and Peace (AALP),
Daund 413801, Poona District.

ISBN: 978-81-8465-503-2

Laser typeset by

ISPCK, Post Box 1585, 1654, Madarsa Road, Kashmere Gate,
Delhi-110006 • *Tel:* 23866323

e-mail: ashish@ispck.org.in • ella@ispck.org.in
website: www.ispck.org.in

Printed at Repro Knowledgecast Limited, Thane

Dedicated
to
Asian Academy for Leadership and Peace

Contents

PART 2
CHRISTIAN LEADERSHIP ROLE

PART 3
DEVELOPING LEADERS AND
LEADERSHIP FOR AN ORGANIZATION

Preface

To be leader is an important job, although it is not easy. Today the world, nations, societies, organizations and church's need – men and women who are not just managers of people, money, and organizations. Leadership is always crucial to the church worldwide. Today it seems to me good leadership is essentially urgent. *We live at a time of first class problems and second class leadership.*

Real leaders are in short supply therefore, every leader today should ask – how can I help and encourage the new leadership? In pursuit of growth and prosperity, we have lost the biblical principles in selecting, training and encouraging right leaders for the churches and its organizations. Throughout the Bible, God was looking for leaders. God invites leaders to lead people to achieve His purpose for example, Moses, Joshua, David, Joseph, Nehemiah, Saul, even He sent his son Jesus Christ.

If leaders are invited by God they will have characteristics like – trust worthy, conviction, competence and charisma. Godly leader will have fruits of the spirit - love, joy, peace, longsuffering, kindness, faithfulness, gentleness and self-control. One can mention the *three components of Christian leadership: character, knowledge and leadership skills.*

Today we need leaders of high calibre, with great quality, character who play a very active and crucial role in the present dynamic society.

My purpose in this book, therefore, is to highlight the qualities and role of Christian leader. I have dealt with leadership characteristics in the first volume. The qualities include: ambition, integrity, trust, courage and confidence, openness, accountability, transparency, commitment, humility, compassion etc. The success of an organization or church largely depends upon the leadership. The role of a Christian leader is unique, because he has to be compassionate like a shepherd and a servant and also spiritual. I have sufficiently discussed the role of a Christian leader in the book.

Many Christian leaders are looking for direction and wondering what is that they are missing. They wonder where to go, they wonder what to do? Certainly leading God's people requires wisdom and a variety of skills. The desire to grow and be equipped as a leader is a right one, but we can often be looking for direction in the wrong places. On the many occasions I looked for information on leadership, I discovered that it is not often easy to find it in one book or two. Therefore, I felt that there is a need, for common laymen, a book that will provide easy access for Christian leadership from different perspectives.

When I was called to lead the Asian Academy for Leadership and Peace, a ministry equipping pastors and leaders, I was influenced by the writings of John Maxwell, Rick Warren and others. Their writings gave me practical resources and ideas for my teaching. This book (volume two) deals with Christian leadership qualities and role. It includes about twenty eight lessons or guidelines for every Christian leader. Volume one deals with Christian Leadership Character and the third volume discusses Biblical Leadership Models. I suggest you to read the first volume to get better understanding of Christian leadership before second and third. The three volumes will be useful for those who aspire to be leaders in church or Christian organizations. However, these books are useful to all Christian leaders at all levels, in the church, home, work place and society.

I don't claim that this book is unique but I tried to deal with important aspects of Christian leadership's qualities and role, as simple as possible. In reality this book consist many author's ideas which have been looked and analysed through my life experience, as a Chairman of Association of Christian Institutes of Social Concern in Asia, Indian Society for Social Action and Asian Academy for Leadership and Peace. Wherever possible I have tried to give credit to the appropriate source. The Word in Life Study Bible has been a great source, which I used after my first draft was completed.

The purpose of this book is: 1. to assist those who are interested in Christian leadership by providing material with endnotes and references. 2. To expose the qualities and role for proper direction. 3. To use this book as a resource material; for resources persons, pastors and participants of various leadership trainings, mainly at Asian Academy for Leadership and Peace.

The journey of Asian Academy for Leadership and Peace has just started and there is a lot to be done in the years to come. I feel the hand of God behind all the success.

I suspect I will not be telling you anything you did not already know. But I do hope that this book will sharpen your thoughts, ideas, skills and abilities. Often readers may ask, what is the point in reading another book on leadership? I feel one should get all the help to be a great leader, I hope this book will answer questions relating to Christian leadership. As Jon Byler says, "read, reflect and respond".

If you love the concept of Christian leadership, make sure you teach the same to others. Begin as a student of Christian leadership, but aim to be a teacher of Christian leadership. Spreading knowledge will increase your knowledge. Believe me, it has worked for me and it will work for you too.

Beyond mere formality or courtesy, I would like to record my thanks for my friends for their support and encouragement. God enabled me to write few books on Industrial Relations, however, this is my first book on Christian leadership. This book is an outcome of the encouragement, I received as a Chairman for Association of Christian Institutes of Social Concern in Asia for 8 years and as a founder and Chairman of Asian Academy for Leadership and Peace, while I organized many seminars/workshops on leadership on various themes in various Asian countries and for Global Oikosnet.

John Zechariah

Introduction

*T*he meaning of quality is the standard of something as measured against similar thing, while character is typical quality of a person or thing. Leadership qualities therefore, includes standard and a typical qualities of a leader, like, be good, better, strong and true, though these traits overlap. Character is the qualities and traits that make up a person, the care of your being, the heart of who you are.

Everyone must be leader. In our lives, we need to remember that someone has influenced and helped to set standard, inspired and motivated to achieve goals. Such persons can be good and true leader. Unfortunately, we lack true leaders today. In spite leaders abuse their power, out of helplessness, we still appoint or elect such leader and even follow in many circumstances, because we need them. We need leaders in all walks of life – to provide new perspective, to inspire to have broader vision, to keep us on track when we are on the wrong side of life,

How can a leader become true leader?

1. A true leader wants nothing more than to make people stand on their own as leaders in their own

> **Welcome the challenges that God sends your way-they will strengthen your character.**

rights. Moses was ashepherd taking care of sheep and also a spokesperson to God. God saw in Moses the character

2. of love, care, humility and the capacity to lead. Therefore, God chose him to lead the Israelites.

3. A leader has to have charisma, respect, sense of authority, selflessness and humility

4. A true leader is servant leader. Jesus Christ humbled himself by washing his disciples feet.

> *Encouragement or inspiration can come from many sources: God's presence, the Bible and other believers.*

5. A leader who inspires with love. Moses inspired his immediate

6. followers and the people of Israelites. Nehemiah was one of the most inspiring leaders in the Bible in building the wall.

7. A true leader helps to understand life and the way it should be led.

8. A true leader does not want followers, they are interested in preparing leaders

9. A true leader does not impose leadership nor take away freedom from his/her team or followers

10. A true leader must be a living example of his/her teaching

11. A true leader will have vision but it has to be translated and applicable. For this they need to have knowledge and communication skills. Only 3to5 per cent of pastors have a compelling vision (Jon Byler).

12. A true leader should be a great visionary with courage, like King David.

Nehemiah exhibited the quality of an initiator. He initiated project to build the wall. He knew what he wanted, he encouraged his people to act, he took risks and he had courage. Leader needs these qualities to be effective and successful even today. The leaders who have qualities of initiators; know what they want, they push themselves to act, they take risks, they make mistakes and do things with courage.

The quality of a leader depends upon, how much he/she understands about leadership.

What is leadership? *"Leadership is influence. Nothing more, nothing less."* Every leader needs to know: leadership is influence, not position. Leaders are significant because they make things happen, everything rises and falls on leadership, it is therefore important to start growing as a leader and growing other leaders (Jon Byler).

Leadership is often understood in terms of power, manipulation, assertiveness and ambition. During Jesus time, the Roman Empire was dominated by very powerful and manipulative family dynasties riddled with competition, violence, greed and dirty politics. But Jesus modelled a different way of leadership. Throughout the New Testament we are shown glimpses of His life and character. In them we discover a stark contrast to our world's soap opera of abuse and distortion. In Hebrew 5 it describes a true leader as:

1. *Focused on people* and how they connect with God.

2. *Compassionate with the weak and ignorant.*

3. *Required to face sin head-on.*

4. *Not self-appointed* but rather called by God into his role.

Leaders welcome the challenges that God sends their way, strengthens their character.

I have presented Leadership Qualities in Part I and Role of Leader in part II.

PART 1

Christian Leadership Qualities

Chapter 1

Ambitious Leader

Leader has to be Ambitious

*A*mbition is a strong desire to achieve and ambitious means determined to succeed. Ambition is defined also "as a cherished desire to serve the world with the highest form of ourselves. It is a mysterious force that emanates from deep within you. There is a magnet that draws you toward certain ideals, activities and organizations. I believe this is a gift. Pay attention to your ambition and identify it" (Nicole Green). *If you wish to reach the highest, begin at the lowest with least authority.*

> "Authority is not the power a boss has over subordinates, but rather the boss's ability to influence subordinates to recognize and accept that power"(Pieter Bruyn)

Humankind is divided into three categories, those that are immovable, and those that move. A leader has to be mover. A leader has to be positive and optimistic. The pessimist says, it cannot be done, the optimist says, it can be done, while strong optimist says, I just did it.

Leaders can be identified with various distinctive ambitions depending on their goals and desires. A successful leader's ambitions should be:

a. Drive to serve people,

b. Drive to be unique and independent.

c. Drive to understand and learn

d. Drive to be true to convictions

e. Drive to use imagination and think outside the box

f. Great CompassionAmbition can be good or bad, depends on how a person uses it. There has to be ambition, but it makes all the difference whether a leader's ambition revolves around the individual or around a selfless cause.

The tower of Babel was not really an attempt to scale the heights of heaven, and it was not for that reason that God was displeased. God was upset because the whole ambitious project was an act of rebellion against him.

A leader cannot have any ambition which is not in harmony with God.

"You can make many plans, but the Lord's purpose will prevail" (Proverbs 19:21)

It is natural for a leader to be ambitious and aspire for greater leadership role. To aspire for leadership is an honourable ambition but for noble, worthy and honourable cause, and with a selfless motivation. God will condemn wrong ambition and motivation and wrong achievement. Christian leaders should not campaign for promotion and fulfil ambitions, but they will succeed if they have the qualities of a leader. True greatness and true leadership is found in leaders who serve others rather than makes others serve. True service never comes without cost and without sacrifices and suffering.

Leadership carries power, prestige and privileges and a good leader always uses these for the greater interest of the team and organization. Every Christian leader is required to develop skills and talents to make life, the team and organization more effective and efficient, and finally fulfil God's call. John Maxwell believes that most people use only about 10 per cent of their potential. Those who use as much as 25 per cent are called geniuses.

Leader carries power but remembers dangers of power. Like fire, power can be used to accomplish good. But always lurking in its shadow is the temptation of abuse, to use power for self-centred gains that harm others and to avoid accountability. Responding to the Roman soldiers who policed Jerusalem, John raised three issues in regard to the abuse of power (Luke 3:14):

1. *Intimidation:* We can use our power to push others around, especially those who are too weak or afraid to push back. Using power in that way is ungodly and harmful. Ultimately such power users destroy themselves, for their subordinates serve them without loyalty and with increasing resentment.

2. *False Accusations:* We can use our power to make snap decisions and judgements. But power used in such a way keeps us in the dark, since others would be too afraid to correct us when we are wrong. When things go away from the expected course or position, it becomes all too easy to start blaming people under us and around us.

3. *Discontent:* If we use our power in self-centred, hurtful ways, we would want to increase our appetite for power and seek more, perhaps by pressuring superiors or by unfair means.

It is necessary to accept a leader's ambition but it should be in harmony with his team and organization.

"Remember, as responsibilities increase rights decrease for a leader".

Anyone can follow a path, but only a leader can blaze one. This is often not easy. If you are a leader, a lot of people depend on you. Two options come with leadership: the temptation to serve yourself and the opportunity to serve the people you lead.

Leadership *'is about service, about shepherd who cares for the sheep.'* The word 'shepherd' communicates the love, nurture and spiritual care a godly leader provides. It involves both the rod (correction) and staff (direction). Psalm 23 describes the shepherd's functions such as: provides necessities, confidently leads, guides and directs, loves unconditionally, protects from harm, corrects and comforts and provides shelter.

Nehemiah chooses to be a servant-leader and it earned him enormous respect.

The characteristics of a servant leader can be summarized.

'Mercy, peace and love be yours in abundance'

"All those who have authority, should use their power to lead;

by taking orders from the Lord and serving those in need (D. De Hann)".

Leaders who serve will serve as good leaders.

Rehoboam crowned as king of Israel after the death of Solomon. The people were burdened by the harsh rule of Solomon and they pleaded with Rehoboam to be kind. Rehoboam consulted senior leaders of Solomon for their advice. The elders advised Rehoboam

If you will be a servant to these people and serve them and give them a favourable service, they will be always be your servants' (Kings 11 and 12).

'Leadership is use of power to serve the people'

The truth is that the best leaders desire to serve others, not themselves.

A true servant leader:

- Puts others ahead of their own agenda
- Possesses the confidence to serve
- Initiates service to others
- Is not position conscious
- Serves out of love

In short, a good Christian leader needs to have qualities like: Visionary, Influencer, Passion infuser, Team builder, Victorious sufferer, Fighter, Helper and giver, Determined Man and Woman of Integrity, Stabilizer, Compromiser, Encourager and Servant-leader.

Let me conclude in the words of Walter C Wright:

"I pray with Paul and Jude, asking God to fill you with the knowledge of his will through all spiritual wisdom and understanding... that you may live a life worthy of the Lord and may please him in every way; bearing fruit in every good work, growing in the knowledge of God, being strengthened with all power according to his glorious might so that you may have great endurance and patience, and joyfully giving thanks to the Father, who has qualified you to share in the inheritance of the saints in the kingdom of light. For he has rescued us from the dominion of darkness and brought us into the kingdom of the Son he loves, in whom we have redemption, the forgiveness of sins, (Col 1:9-14)

To him who is able to keep you from falling and to present you before his glorious presence without fault and with great joy — to the only God our Saviour be glory, majesty, power and authority, through Jesus Christ our Lord, before all ages, now and forevermore! Amen. (Jude 24-25)

Leaders are prepared for a specific purpose or task, considering the place and size of their team or organization. Jesus did not follow such factors. He chooses and trained His disciples for the mission He wanted them to carry. Successful leaders will have natural and spiritual qualities. J. Oswald Sanders suggests that leaders need to have qualities such as: discipline, vision, wisdom, clear and swift decision power, moral and physical courage, humility, integrity, sincerity, sense of humour, anger (positive), patience, friendship, tact and diplomacy, inspiration power, executive ability, the therapy of listening, and art of writing.The real and authentic Christian character is formed when you surrender to Christ and allow His work to grow under His guidance and spirit.

Aspiring to a leadership position is a good thing. There is a difference between stepping forward to accept the responsibility of leadership and stepping forward to put oneself into the spotlight for the benefit of self-promotion. When a person has the opportunity to lead, serve well with all your abilities, but you cannot force yourself into the position. Wait for God's call as Moses waited for 40 years. The road to Christian leadership depends upon service.

"Don't work yourself into the spotlight; don't push your way to the place of prominence. It's better to be promoted to a place of honour than face humiliation by being demoted (Proverbs 25:6-7)

Jesus knew that every great achievement required a willingness to begin small. Ambitious leader, remember everything big, starts little. Whatever you have been given is enough to create anything you have been promised. Whatever you possess today is enough to create anything else you will ever want in your future. Jesus began his life in a stable. David had a slingshot, but he became a king. Joseph was sold as a slave, but he became Prime Minister of Egypt.[1]

Chapter 2

Uncompromised Integrity in both Words and Actions[1]

Living with integrity requires personal sacrifice, but the eternal rewards outweigh whatever we give up in this life.

*I**ntegrity means quality of being morally good.* Integrity is about holistic honesty, and consistency in character. Values and beliefs depend on the character of integrity, an individual cannot show integrity selectively, and otherwise he/she will not have followers. Person is a good leader, if their actions; inspire others to dream more, learn more, do more and achieve more.

> *The integrity of the upright guides them, but the unfaithful are destroyed by their duplicity.* (Proverbs 11:3)

Integrity means honesty and more. It refers to having strong internal guiding principles that one does not compromise. It also means treating others as you would wish to be treated. Integrity is the quality of being morally good. *Integrity is a quality which includes-honesty, dependability, uprightness, loyalty and sincerity.* Integrity springs from an individual's ethical and spiritual convictions

Leaders are regularly battered by circumstances, by Satan, and by their own people. All good leaders must demonstrate that they can take it without losing composure. People are drawn to strength of character, and tend to believe what strong people say. While they may feel sympathetic toward the weak, they tend not to follow them. This does not mean leaders should pretend they are not suffering, but that their determination and integrity dictate that they maintain consistency even in the face of suffering. It also means that a leader would continue to pursue the right goals and live for God even if no one else follows.

It is believed that a solid sense of right and wrong and strong guiding principles are the most essential and basic leadership character or skill. Integrity is skill to the extent that we see in action. A good leader is not afraid of rejection by his followers because the concern is doing what is right, not being followed. Jesus taught that the good shepherd "goes out before them," which means that such a shepherd sets a course knowing that the sheep will follow after. When people sense that a leader is more concerned about being followed than about what God wants, they grow cynical about following them. Most people are suspicious of leaders anyway, and will test leaders by threatening not to follow. Only when they see that a leader cannot be manipulated will they realize that their choice is to follow or to take their chances elsewhere. Integrity is equally important in big and small things. Any break in moral principles can create crack in leadership integrity.

Integrity is the most important ingredient in leadership. A leader needs to understand integrity well, and develop and practice it to be successful. Being a person of integrity means, to do what you know is true. Many times leaders try to change another person's behaviour while having the same problem themselves. People of integrity watches their words carefully and make sure that whatever they preach, they practice. If they preach humility and honesty, they should show that they practice it as well. Integrity promotes trust and not much is accomplished without trust.

Noah was a righteous man. He loved God with his whole heart and was honest to God's call. From Noah's life we can learn that it is possible to be faithful, honest and please God even in the midst of a corrupt and sinful generation. Surely it was not easy for Noah but he obeyed sincerely and honestly.

Paul spoke of his failures and success with openness, only few leaders practice these days. Even before his conversion he served God sincerely and with great integrity (2 Timothy 1:3) and with great personal integrity. Integrity and sincerity are qualities of leadership, and were part of God's law for the Israelites (Deuteronomy 18:13). God wants His people to show transparent character.

David wrote this prayer

"May integrity and uprightness protect me, because my hope is in you?" (Psalms 25:21).

Solomon says

"He who walks in integrity walks securely."

"You must always act in the fear of the Lord, with integrity and with undivided hearts" (2 Chronicles 19:9)

Therefore, integrity is sincerity of heart and intention, truthfulness, uprightness, being sincere, honest and pure heart in all your intentions.

Joseph was also a man of integrity with high moral character. Joseph refused his master's wife's desire to go to bed with her, the consequence was painful and ultimately prison. A leader can learn more than one lesson here. Joseph was honest to his master, sincere in his duty and not tempted or attracted for physical pleasure.

Paul was a determined leader even while he was in prison, he shared the gospel.

Paul showed his high degree of integrity while he criticized his fellow believer Peter. He criticized Peter's hypocrisy and demanded that all Christian leaders remain consistent, regardless of the company they keep. From Paul we can learn lesson on criticism.[1]

- *Check your motive before your criticism. The goal should be to help not humiliate.*

- *Make sure the issue is worthy of criticism.*

- *Be specific. Don't drop hints, but clearly name the problem.*

- *Don't undermine the person's self-confidence or identity. Make it obvious that you value the person.*

- *Do not postpone needed criticism. If the same is big, act now.*

- *Look at yourself looking at others. Take the log out of your own eye.*

- *End criticism with encouragement. Finish on a positive note.*

Very few leaders have the courage to invite their followers to evaluate their leadership like Job.

> *"Teach me, and I will be quiet; show me where I have been wrong"* (Job 6:24).

> The best way to deal with your failures is to humbly learn from them and move on.

Only a leader with strong character and a strong sense of security, positive motive and conscience can do this. A leader must be strong enough to admit mistakes, smart enough to learn from them, and strong enough to correct them.

How many Christian leaders have this kind of character – integrity?

> "For people, who hate discipline and only get more stubborn, there will come a day when life tumbles in and they break, but by then it will be too late to help them" *(Proverbs 29:1)*.

Many leaders ruined their lives and damaged others' lives because of lack of integrity. Character becomes crucial issue in a leader's life. It is necessary to strike balance between character and

> If you ignore criticism, you will end in poverty and disgrace; if you accept criticism, you will be honoured. (Proverbs 13:18)

ability, of course both are necessary for development. John Maxwell has shown how to balance:[2]

What I am	What I do	What I can
Humble	Rely on God	Power from God
Visionary	Set Goals	High Morale
Convicted	Do the Right Thing	Credibility

It is better to look at the future than past. Never build future around your past. God never sees your past to decide your future. Stop looking at where you were or have been but start looking at where you are going. While leaders try to maintain integrity, they have to overcome questionable background. Jesus overcame the stigma of a questionable background-His birth.

> *"Brothers, I do not consider myself yet to have taken hold of it. But one thing I do: Forgetting what is behind and straining toward what is ahead, I press on toward the goal to win the prize for which God has called me heavenward in Christ Jesus."* (Philippines 3:13-14)

Daniel in the Den of Lion is the finest example of honesty and integrity; he exemplified trusting and praying to God without the fear of death. When the King saw Daniel alive without any harm, he was overjoyed and gave orders to lift Daniel out of the den. King ordered decree in every part of his kingdom that people must fear and worship the God of Daniel. (Daniel 6)

Jehu accepted God's command and destroyed the house of Ahab and the worship of Baal. God commended Jehu for his brilliant way of fulfilling His mission. God blessed him for his obedience. However, Jehu compromised his devotion to God by leaving intact some idols from Israel's past. Even after great success, Jehu took no heed to walk in the law of the Lord God of Israel with all his heart. Jehu accomplished great things for the Lord and the kingdom of Israel, but his compromise led to another vile form of idolatry. In the end, his disobedience overshadowed his accomplishment as a leader.[3]

Compassion and integrity, regarding money in a leader's life is very crucial (1 Corinthians 16: 1-4). Money is powerful, it can bring out the best or the worst in a person or in a leader, to drive to gain a lot of it or use it for personal comfort and convenience, we can become very cold and manipulate. But that ought not to be the way for God's followers.

Paul pointed out that the transfer of the funds would be carried out by responsible people chosen by the Corinthians themselves. This guaranteed accountability and integrity.

Integrity of words or keeping promises and action of a leader is very important (2 Samuel 9:1-13).Scripture presents David as a leader who kept his promises. David had sworn that he would show kindness to Jonathan's descendants. So once he was installed as king, David asked whether any of Saul's descendants remained alive. Jonathan's son Mephibosheth was found and David kept his promise (2 Samuel 9:7-13).

This incident stands as a challenge to God's people (leaders) today to follow through on their promises. Sometimes it's easy to rationalize a way out of keeping faith, especially when circumstances and relationship change. Yet David kept his commitment, even though Jonathan's father spent years trying to take David's life. David knew that God took the covenant between him and Jonathan seriously. David was therefore, determined to follow through.

David's example also challenges parents and grandparents to uphold commitments made by earlier generations. To do so is a marvellous legacy to pass on to one's children. It reflects the truth that we serve a promise-keeping God.

Leader has to observe or practice integrity in daily living (Psalms 15:2). Many people would like to enjoy close, personal relations with God. But such intimacy begins with a lifestyle of integrity. David lists several criteria for assessing one's character. Significantly, almost all of them relate to workplace issues.

Psalms 15 presents a summary of what God expects of His people (especially leaders). The question under discussion is who is good enough to meet with God?

The answer is interesting in that rather than giving a list of does's and don'ts, this psalm describe godliness in terms of character. *The qualities extend to personal issues of integrity and honesty, our relationship with others, and the way we handle our money.*

Psalms 15 anticipates another list of qualities that matter to God, Jesus teaching on what are called the Beatitudes (Matthew 5:3-12). Of all the virtues Christ commended in the Beatitudes, it is significant that the first is humility, being "poor in spirit". That underlines all the others.

Leader's great qualities include integrity and honesty. What is honesty? *Honesty is the quality or fact of being honest; uprightness and fairness, truthfulness, sincerity, or frankness, freedom from deceit or fraud.* If a ruler pays attention to lies, all his servants become wicked (Proverbs 29:12). *Remember lying leads to trouble.* Leaders who stand for the truth can become unpopular.

Discerning truth from falsehood is a continuing challenge for those in authority. There are several reasons for this:

1. Subordinates often have a personal agenda.

2. Subordinates are generally reluctant to tell their superiors bad news.

3. Subordinates are generally reluctant to voice ideas or opinions with which they think their bosses are likely to disagree.

4. People often see the same thing in different ways.

Given these realities, perhaps the leader's greatest challenge is to create an atmosphere in which truth and openness are respected, encouraged and rewarded. If you are in a position of authority, can you list three ways in which you encourage the people under you to be honest? Or do you just assume they will be? Do they see honesty demonstrated in your treatment of them?[4]

Bible highlights the significance of integrity from various perspectives, very valuable to every Christian and mainly to Christian leader:

1. God rejoices in the integrity of his people

2. Integrity is essential for leaders

3. Integrity takes effort and discipline

4. God watches over people with integrity

5. Leaders prove their integrity at home

6. Leaders in the church must have integrity

7. We must maintain integrity in teaching others

Chapter 3

Striving Hard to Earn Trust

*T*rust means firm belief in the reliability, truth, or ability of someone or something. Leader should strive hard to earn trust and also trust colleagues in an organization, because trust is fundamental in building strong relationships to fulfil vision, mission and goals. Without trust small issues become big and affect relationships, efficiency and effectiveness. As trust grows, the relationships grow strong and big issues/problems become non-issues and open an opportunity to tackle the problems brings positive result.

"And Abraham believed the Lord, and the Lord counted him as righteous because of his faith" (Genesis 15:6).

It was by faith that Abraham obeyed, when God called time to leave home and go to another land that God would give him as his inheritance. He went without knowing where he was going (Hebrews 11:8-12).

It was by faith that even Sarah was able to have a child, though she was barren and was too old. She believed that God would keep his promise.

David said can someone give me a drink of the water from the well of Bethlehem. Immediately three mighty men broke through the camp of the Philistines, drew water from the well of Bethlehem that was not in their region, and brought water to David. These three men took risk of their life and crossed to Philistine, because David had earned their trust, love and loyalty. David honoured their sacrifice by presenting the water to the Lord. As a leader, do you have such followers or have earned such trust from your team.

Trust is crucial in leadership; in fact it is the basis of good leadership. Before David became king he respected and trusted king Saul and he prospered with God's blessings. Saul failed to practice the trust and respect; therefore, he lost his kingdom.

A leader can trust God like the prophet Habakkuk.

Though the fig tree does not bud and there are no grapes on the vines, though the olive crop fails and the fields produce no food, though there are no sheep in the pen and no cattle in the stalls, yet I will rejoice in the LORD, I will be joyful in God my saviour. The Sovereign LORD is my strength; he makes my feet like the feet of a deer, he enables me to go on the heights. (Habakkuk 3: 17-19)

From this passage leader can learn three lessons:

1. Habakkuk commits to praising God regardless of external circumstances

2. Habakkuk praises God specifically for salvation

3. Habakkuk recognizes the Lord as His strength.

Habakkuk trusted God even during the most difficult times. Like Habakkuk, can leaders choose and praise God even while facing desolation. Leader need to draw strength from God with trust in Him.

Chapter 4

Courage and Self-Confidence to do the Right Thing

The greatest test of courage on earth is to bear defeat without losing heart.
Often the test of courage is not to die but to live.
A man of courage is also full of faith.
Life shrinks or expands in proportion to your courage.
Great things are done more through courage than through wisdom

Anonymous

*C*ourage is a quality of mind which enables one to encounter dangerous difficulties with firmness or without fear or failing of heart, valour, and boldness. Confidence means freedom from doubt, belief in you. Courage is also defined as bravery. The opposite of courage is to submit to fear. Courage is an essential ingredient to establish leadership. There are different kinds of courage – moral, spiritual, spontaneous and unprepared courage.

Courage is a prime requisite of leadership. Lord Moran, personal physician to Sir Winston Churchill found soldiers who could be placed broadly in one of four categories.[1] *Men who did not feel fear.*

1. Men who felt fear but did not show it.

2. Men who felt fear, showed it, but did their job.

3. Men, who felt fear, showed it and shirked.

> It is better to trust the Lord than to put confidence in people. It is better to trust the Lord than put confidence in princes.(Psalm 118:8-9)

"Be strong and of good courage" (Deuteronomy 31:7).

"Be on guard. Stand true to what you believe. Be courageous. Be Strong." (1 Corinthians 16:13)

Leaders, who act boldly during crisis and changes, will find followers. Courage is willingness to overcome fear and plan to move ahead. Courage, confidence and decisiveness are most important qualities of Christian leader. Lack of courage, demonstrate weakness and delay in decision making, which might invite problems. Courage means ability to control fear when facing danger or pain. Courage can be defined as the ability and commitment to endure and challenge difficulty or danger with firmness in spite of fear. A good leader derives courage from the fear of God and exhibits it at the right time. Today, we need leaders of courage, who knows when to fear and when he should not. Courage is significant for the development and success of an organization. Courageous decision should be wise, because it involves challenge.

John Maxwell suggests the following truths about courage:[2]

- *Courage begins with an inward battle.*

- Courage is making thing right, not just smoothing them over.

- Courage in a leader inspires commitment from followers. Courage by a leader inspires.

- Your life expands in proportion to your courage.

Whenever we see progress in an organization, it is because the leader took courageous decisions. Courage gives leadership position. As you approach toward tough decisions that will challenge you, you will recognize truths.

A leader in an organization is not always the smartest or most creative person on the team. He is also not necessarily the first to identify an opportunity. The leader is the one who has the courage to initiate to set things in motion and move ahead.

David can be the best example when he showed his courage, capability, strong confidence and made the right decision to fight Goliath. God gave him victory and David in turn gave Him all the credit and glory. David exhibited his bravery and gave an entire army something that was lacking - courage. David was courageous and careful in taking risk. No leader can be

> God promises to give you all the courage and strength you need to live for him.

successful without taking risk. Leader cannot take risk without courage; therefore, courage is essential for leadership.

Courage and confidence should come from God. David said to the Philistine (Goliath)

> "You come against me with sword and spear and javelin, but I come against you in the name of the LORD Almighty, the God of the armies of Israel, whom you have defied. This day the LORD will hand you over to me, and I'll strike you down and cut off your head. Today I will give the carcasses of the Philistine army to the birds of the air and the beasts of the earth, and the whole world will know that there is a God in Israel. (1 Samuel 17:45-46)

David was triumphant over the Philistines because of his courage, confidence in God, and took the right decision and the right time. Help is largely given to people of courage. One of the greatest pleasures of life is doing the things that others say you cannot do. I am sure

> Be on guard. Stand true to what you believe. Be courageous. Be strong. (I Corinthians 15:13)

David experienced the greatest pleasure after he killed Goliath.

God said to Moses:

> Be strong and courageous. Do not be afraid or terrified because of them, for the Lord your God goes with you, he will never leave you nor forsake you."

Then Moses summoned Joshua and said to him in the presence of all Israel,

> Be strong and courageous, for you must go with this people into the land that the Lord swore to their forefathers to give them, and you must divide it among them as their inheritance. The Lord himself goes before you and will be with you; he will never leave you nor forsake you. Do not be afraid, do not be discouraged

Here we see that Moses and Joshua both had courage and confidence to follow God's order. (Deuteronomy 31:6-8)

Nehemiah develops courage and confidence and made clear decisions to build wall of Jerusalem. People ridiculed him but he was determined to build the wall. Like already mentioned, one of the greatest pleasures of life is doing the things that others say you cannot do; this I say with my experience when I started Indian Society for Social Action and its institutions. Abraham and Sarah left Ur full of hope and confidence that God will guide them.

Esther was willing to break Persian protocol and walk into the king's presence with confidence and hope.

These people were able to accomplish what they wished, because of courage, hope and confidence.

Paul says to Corinthians,

> *"Be on your guard, stand firm in the faith, be men of courage, be strong. Do everything in love"* (1 Corinthians 16:13-14).

A man of courage is also full of faith like Paul.

The following night the Lord stood near Paul and said,

"Take courage! As you have testified me in Jerusalem, so you must also testify in Rome" (Acts 23:11).

Often the test of courage is not to die but to live. A Christian leader needs to do what is right in the sight of God, despite what his followers say or believe. Faith, hope, charity, all the rest don't become virtue until it takes courage to exercise them.

> **Dream what you dare to dream.**
> **Go where you want to go.**
> **Be what you want to be.**
> **Believe in yourself and others will too**

God said to Jacob, So do not fear, for I am with you; do not be dismayed, for I am your God. I will strengthen you and help you; I will uphold you with my righteous right hand. (Isaiah 41:10)

Andy Stanley[3] suggests three expressions of courage that often elude leaders:

1. The courage to say no
2. Courage to face current reality
3. Courage to dream

Every leader is mostly aware of what is the right thing to do, yet for convenience and personal benefit, they commit for wrong things in their leadership. Leaders need courage to do the right thing; this will bring respect, satisfaction, strength, peace of mind and help to build trust which is very crucial for a leader. Courage and boldness are two sides of the same coin. Courage speaks of leader's character, while boldness is personality. Boldness also means confidence of leader, what one speaks and does. For Christian leader courage, confidence and boldness comes from God.

"...and they were all filled with the Holy Spirit and spoke the word of God boldly" (Acts 4: 31)

A leader is expected to have courage and self-confidence to do what is right. Jesus committed himself to fulfil God's plan, for which he had courage and did the right thing. When a leader is committed to the right thing, they may have to pay a price, like Jesus went on the cross. A leader who wishes to do the right thing needs to be a disciplined thinker, disciplined in their emotions and take disciplined action. A leader also needs to be obedient, self-controlled, and obey rules and regulations to do the right thing.

No one prepares for war without courage and confidence, and war has to have just cause. Moses, Joshua and Nehemiah had courage, confidence and were convinced that they were doing the right thing.

An effective leader works for real value or significant work, and with the right attitude.

If a leader wants to establish credibility and gain confidence, he has to fulfil promises and commitments without fail. If for some reason they cannot, they should feel to express their inability with reason.

Leader has to be careful about what they promise. Do not make unnecessary promise to God or/and people. Solomon identifies three pitfalls of a leader – hasty speech, empty promises and lame excuses.[4]Moses was always confident in fulfilling his promises, therefore, he earned credibility, even while Israelites disobeyed him on many occasion. Earning credibility is not easy. A leader's main job is to fulfil promises. The important principles a leader has to remember – harmonious relationship, clear vision, sincere commitment and faith in God, like Moses.

A leader has to pay price for commitment. King Hezekiah did what was good and right and true before God.

Thus Hezekiah did throughout all Judah, and he did what was good and right and the Lord his God. And in every work that he began in the service of the house of God, in the law and in the commandment, to seek his God, he did it with all his heart. So he prospered. (2 Chronicles 31:20-21).

After all that King Hezekiah had so faithfully done, Sennacherib king of Assyria came and invaded Judah. At the end God blessed Hezekiah and saved him from war because he was committed for God's purpose.

When leaders honour and commit to God's call, He moves and events follow. Ruth chose to stay with Naomi, her mother-in- law, even after she lost her husband. Her commitment opened new doors of opportunity for her and she found a new husband – Boaz.

According to Ken Blanchard,

"...there is difference between interest and commitment. When you are interested in doing something, you do it only when it is convenient. When you are committed to something, you accept no excuse."[5]

Commitment is a pre-requisite for a successful leadership. Without commitment there can be no success.

God promises to give you all the courage and strength you need to live. Therefore, pray for courage. Courage helps us to boldly represent Christ (Acts 4:31) because He ultimately gives us success.

Chapter 5

Conflict with Openness

Conflict resolution is possible when you turn to God for help
Accept the constructive criticism that can help you grow,
then forget about the rest

*C*onflict means a serious disagreement or argument. It is a state of mind in which a person experiences a clash of opposing feelings or needs. It is also defined as a serious incompatibility between two or more people. Openness can be said as allowing access or not closed or blocked.

One of the great qualities of a true leader is an open and balanced mind and having a diplomatic approach to tackle confronting and conflicting issues. If there is no dealing with conflicting and confronting issues for long time, it will have adverse effects, and may eventually result into failure of leadership and organization. Failure is the opportunity to begin again, more intelligently. – Henry Ford

Leadership and conflict are part of a leader's life and they go hand in hand. Handling conflict is part of leadership responsibility. Conflict is inevitable in a group or organization. Therefore, a leader has to have ability to manage conflicts.

Why do conflicts arise?

Hsin-Yi Cohen[1] explains, "Conflict often develops due to poor communication, lack of openness and weak leadership. It can also arise when there is dissatisfaction with the leadership style, especially after a change in leadership, with certain members seeking power." He also mentions signs of conflicts:

> Dear friends, don't be surprised at the fiery trials you are going through, as if something strange were happening to you. Instead, be very glad-because these trials will make you partners with Christ in his suffering, and afterward you will have the wonderful joy sharing his glory when it is displayed to the entire world. (I Peter 4:12-13)

- Constant disagreement between team members
- An increasing lack of respect between the members
- Strong and negative public statements,
- Lack of honesty
- Lack of clear goals
- Poor communication between team members
- Negative body language.

Relationship is crucial in managing conflicts. If conflicts are managed with openness, relationships will be at stake. It is essential that leaders handle conflicts with a positive, creative and productive mind. Stronger relations can bring stronger impact and peace in an organization. Communication can bring transformation in relationships and positively convert conflict into opportunity.

According to Richard Branson,[2] a true and successful leader needs to master how to handle conflicts:

1. Stay out of the conflict, stay in serenity and remain flexible and open.
2. Recognize what is underneath the conflict.

3. Transform the conflict into an opportunity.

Art of self-motivation will bring major impacts on leadership as per Richard Branson.[3]

1. A healthy relationship with self.

2. Productive relationships to others.

3. Authentic leadership connected to purpose.

It is vital that leaders know how to manage the conflict and bring peace, because conflict can be destructive. A skilful leader can resolve conflicts. Hsin-YiCohen[4] gives the following tips to handle conflicts:

1. Don't make conflict personal.

2. Consider others perspective.

3. Take responsibility and be honest.

Seek reconciliation with others through power of Christ.

4. Don't avoid conflicts.

5. Don't forget to remind everyone that it can be healthy to agree to disagree.

Resolving conflicts calls for openness of a leader and team members. Everyone is responsible in a team to bring peace or resolve the conflict and not just the leader. A leader has to be watchful for every member and listen from their perspective carefully with open mind. Leaders also observe every member whether they listen and respect others' views and are open. Leaders must ensure that all perspectives are respected.

Contact the person directly with whom you have a conflict. This is what the Bible says.

> If your brother sins against you, go and show him his fault, just between the two of you. If he listens to you, you have won your brother over. (Matthew 18:15)

Biblical principle believes, that a third person should not involve at the first stage, as this might lead to gossiping or luring one side or other.

Scripture suggests.

But if he will not listen, take one or two others along, so that 'every matter may be established by the testimony of two or three witnesses.' (Matthew 18:15)

1. Sit face to face with the other party in the conflict with genuine desire to resolve.

2. State your desire to resolve the conflict.

3. Do it without accusing or blaming.

4. If necessary, begin with apology for your role in the conflict.

5. Take responsibility of your share in the conflict.

6. Provide every person chance to speak without interruption or correction.

7. Listening is key to Biblical resolution.

All Biblical leaders like Moses, Joshua, Solomon, David addressed their problems and conflicts with sound mind and along God's directions. Therefore, they were successful. Can Christian leaders today follow their footsteps? Yes, they can!

A large number of conflicts can be avoided by a leader, if he/she accepts constructive criticism. If criticism is ignored, it end in poverty and disgrace, but if one accepts criticism, he/she will be honoured (Proverbs 13:18).

Chapter 6

Accountability, Transparency and Commitment

The quality of your life will largely depend on your commitment
to excellence regardless of your endeavour
A commitment is a living thing not a dormant activity

Accountability means responsibility to someone or for some activity. Commitment is a trait of sincere and steadfast purpose. Commitment can mean the act of binding yourself, intellectually or emotionally to a course of action. Transparency means the quality or state of being transparent.

What is accountability?

According to Richard J. Krejcir

> "It is a check and balance system to protect us from harm from ourselves and others. We do this by being open to what we are thinking and doing so we can receive encouragement and reproof, when needed."

> If you are faithful in the small things, God will trust you with greater responsibilities.

Everyone wants to be leader; however, few are prepared to accept accountability. Leadership and accountability are two sides of the same coin. It is necessary that all leaders be accountable and also be model for others. A leader who is not accountable will fail.

Accountability is more than responsibility. In accountability a leader owns his/her actions, decisions, commitments and also results, good or bad, whereas responsibility means, a leader's duties and role he/she is expected to fulfil. Accountability allows us to be answerable to one another. As a Christian leader, one is also responsible for every action to God.

David violated divine law and strained his character by his sin, against Uriah and by the deceitful way he gained this gallant soldier's wife. David's confession before God is sign of accountability

Jehoash's dealing with priests concerning temple repairs is a useful lesson in accountability (2 Kings 12:6-8). Jehoash delegated specific responsibilities to the priests with clear instructions concerning the collection and use of money. He personally confronted the priests, including their leader, Jehoiada, for their non-performance. He suggested a course of remedial action and then saw to it that an alternative solution to the problem would be carried.

Accountability involves far more than simply telling someone what to do and then coming back later to see if instructions have been carried out. It means that a leader commits to overseeing the workers' performance and making sure that the project is completed.

Leader's ultimate performance depends upon his accountability (1 Corinthians 3:13-15). People often joke about standing before God and having their lives examined. But the picture Paul paints is anything but funny. *He is serious about a day of accountability for the believers.* Most of us are familiar with performance reviews on the job. Paul describes ultimate performance review – the moment when we stand before God and He evaluates the worth of our lives on the earth, not for salvation but for reward or loss.

To achieve best, work ethics and personal excellence are necessary. Steadfast work ethics demands the leader to be honest even when he confronts problems, stress and uncertainty.

Leader's Commitment

Commitment is crucial in every leader's life, of course not based on emotions but on character. Commitment to mission, vision and goals of the organization he/she is a part of, is above all requirements. God's blessings will flow once a leader commits. Ruth chooses to follow her mother-in-law, Naomi even after her husband died. Because of Ruth's commitment, God opened doors of opportunities in a foreign land, finds new husband, Boaz. (Ruth 1:16)

People including leaders often associate commitment with their emotion. Jesus' disciples were full of emotions but not fully committed to their leader. True commitment does not depend on emotions. Our emotions fluctuate, but commitment has to be rock solid. John Maxwell gives a few tips for a leader to know about being committed: commitment is discovered amid adversity, commitment does not depend on abilities, and commitment comes as a result of choice not conditions, and commitment lasts when it is based on value.1 Remember commitment towards vision comes first in leader's life. Nehemiah accomplished the toughest task in building the wall of Jerusalem because of his strong commitment, of course with his people's participation. Leader who wishes to complete his/her task well in time needs,[2]

- Compelling purpose
- Clear perspective
- Continual prayer
- Courageous persistence

And I tell you this, that you must give an account on judgment day of every idle word you speak. (Matthew 12:30)

Commitment is the one quality above all others that enables a potential leader to become a successful leader.

Leader will have to give account for your every word and action, so it is important to live each day for the Lord.

And I tell you this, that you must give an account on judgment day of every idle word you speak (Matthew 12:36)

Yes, each of us will have to give a personal account to God. So don't condemn each other anymore. Decide instead to live in such a way that you will not put an obstacle in another Christian's path (Romans 14:12-13)

What is transparency?

Transparency means the quality or state of being transparent. Everyone can have his definition of transparency. Being transparent means the person realizes that in order for people to have healthy relationships, they need to be able to first have someone they trust and respect to confide with and share their deep serious struggles with. Leaders need not be afraid to share in group settings, about how God is teaching them and working in their life. Transparency also means to air out problems and weakness, and also be willing to share major struggles with all in a team or organization.

Today, transparency and accountability are needed everywhere, from statutory to organization. Transparency has become a buzzword. A transparent leader will always talk straight, show openness and would be accountable for every action, practice integrity, be honest and be an efficient communicator. A leader with great credibility should speak truth and show confidence and positivity. Honesty and truthfulness will make a leader transparent. Honest and truthfulness means being straight and honest with others and doing what is right.

For we are taking pains to do what is right, not only in the eyes of the Lord but also in the eyes of men. (2 Corinthians 8:21)

Therefore, each of you must put off falsehood and speak truthfully to his neighbour, for we are all members of one body. (Ephesians 4:25)

Leadership always comes with a price tag, fear of failure, and honesty and truthfulness.

Most leaders start with great expectations. Unfortunately, in the workplace, whether Christian or not, it is not always welcome to be transparent and open for dialogue. In reality, at least on some occasions, leader can lose job, for being open and transparent.

Joshua's example is worth emulating today. He handled his responsibility/transparency well while he distributed land among the 12 tribes. When Israel divided Canaan, it was Joshua's job to act somewhat like a trustee of an estate, making sure that each tribe received the lands to which it was entitled. It was a delicate job that required him to act with

> Yes, each of us will have to give a personal account to God. So don't condemn each other anymore. Decide instead to live in such a way that you will not put an obstacle in another Christian's path. Romans 14:12-13

great integrity. Otherwise, he would have been charged with being unfair or not transparent in assigning boundaries or with neglecting commitments previously made by Moses.

Joshua handled his responsibility by seeking the welfare of the 12 tribes first, before asking for land himself. In doing so, he ran the risk of having to settle for a leftover, second best portion of Canaan, but avoided any question of impropriety and transparency.

Joshua's example is worth practicing today. As we accept responsibilities and make decisions that affect others, our challenge is to do the right thing by seeking justice, trusting God to work out the details of our own welfare.

Chapter 7

Authentic Humility[1]

Don't be selfish, don't try to impress others.
Be humble, thinking of others as better than you. Philippians 2:3
Humility and repentance are essential for entering God's kingdom.

*H*umility means a humble feeling, a lack of false pride and arrogance. *Humility means the quality of being humble. Humility also means willingness to work with others, encouraging and appreciating.* Through humility, a leader respects his/her followers by, being kind to them.

Humility is an essential character of a Christian leader. Jesus said he who desires to be the greatest in the kingdom must be a servant to all. (Matthew 20:26).

Clothe yourselves with humility toward one another, because God opposes the proud but gives grace to the humble. (1 Peter 5:5)

God's view of greatness is different than what most of the world thinks. The path to true greatness begins with humility.

What is humility?[2]

The meaning of humility in the Bible is one of strength not weakness. Some think that, being humble means we are no good. This is not the picture that the Bible depicts. God says that when you are humble;

you are free from pride and arrogance. A person does not need to defend themself when they understand the Bible's picture of humility, for they know who they are in Christ. They are able to be a peacemaker without needing to fight for their rights. They are able to walk humbly in the power of God's Holy Spirit, not their own personal. Godly humility is comfortable (loving others) with who they are in the Lord and therefore putting others first. Jesus gave good example of humility in action. He was humble and also strong.

I am gentle and humble in heart. (Matthew 11:29)

A gentle answer turns away wrath, but a harsh word stirs up anger. (Proverbs 15:1)

Leadership equals to humility. (Luke 22: 24-27)

When leaders practice humility in action, they gain or enjoy power of humility as per Doug Britton:

1.   You can defuse arguments when you are humble.

2.   You can handle unfair treatment peacefully when you are humble.

3.   You do not have to put on a "false front" when you are humble.

4.   You can eat "humble pie" without being crushed when you are humble.

5.   You can ask forgiveness when you are humble.

6.   You can talk with the right attitude when you are humble.

7.   When you are humble you are likely to have more influence than when you fight.

John Ruskin said, "I believe that the first test of a truly great man is his humility. I don't mean by humility, doubt of his power. But really great men have a curious feeling that the greatness is not of them, but through them. And they see something divine in every other man and are endlessly, foolishly, incredibly merciful."

God wants leaders to be humble and a servant leader. Followers expect leaders to work with them, encourage and appreciate their contribution. *The opposite of humility is pride. Pride is a liability and humility brings benefit.*

When leaders lose humility, they invite arrogance. Leaders have to balance with power and humility. David is the best example of power, confidence and humility. David saw his own weakness with humility and with the fear of God. Acknowledging God's role and giving credit to God is a sign of humility. Leaders need to accept humility and acknowledge that all the abilities, talents and gifts are from God. The one who understands this will never be proud. Humility also means that a person recognizes their strengths and weaknesses.

Out of pride, leaders commit mistakes like David did after he own victory over the Philistines. David chose to listen to Satan, stopped trusting God for the defence of his nation, and undertook a census. David said to Joab and commanders of the troops. "Go and count the Israelites from Beer-Sheba to Dan. Then report back to me so that I may know how many there are. (1 Chronicles 21:2)Most leaders try to hide their failures but David repented and asked God not to punish his people but himself. Good leaders take responsibility of their mistakes. David says, "Was not I who commanded the people to be numbered? I am the one who has sinned and done evil indeed, but these sheep, what have they done? Let your hand, I pray, O Lord my God, be against me and my father's house, but not against people, that they should be plagued." (1 Chronicles 21:17).

Jesus himself humbled by showing servant nature by washing his disciples' feet. The cross comes before the crown; the person who seeks honour will ultimately be humiliated, but the person who humbles himself will later be honoured. Before honour comes humility.

Jesus was the perfect example of humility in the New Testament while Moses was in the Old Testament.

Now Moses was a very humble man, more humble than anyone else on the face of the earth. (Numbers 12:3)

Moses was a powerful man, but he was also a humble man because he saw himself in the light of God and sought God's honour and reputation, not his own.

Kenneth Boa[3] clearly mentioned the qualities of a humble leader:

1. Quality of true humility is a teachable spirit

2. Humble people will be willing to seek wise counsel

3. Humble people are willing to be under authority

> The higher we are placed, the more humbly should we walk?
>
> The essence of being human is that one does not seek perfection.

Forgiveness is another great quality of a leader. As Jesus taught, forgiveness is for everyone, for everything and to be given as often as needed. Jon Byler mentions five results of forgiveness:

1. Reconciliation with God;

2. Reconciliation with others

3. Christian growth;

4. Strengthened prayer life; and

5. Freedom from negative emotions

All leaders make mistakes; this is a part of life. True greatness of a leader lies in accepting and admitting mistakes with humility, rather than blaming others. The best way to deal with failures is to humbly learn from them and move on. The leaders who are willing to own their actions and are honest with their people will be admired, respected and earn the trust of people. A quiet spirit can overcome even great mistakes (Ecclesiastes 10:4)

In washing the disciples' feet, Jesus demonstrated that the son of man was the servant of men; that whatsoever was arrogant, assertive, dogmatic, belonged to the gospel of power, not to his gospel of love. Humility is not just virtuous but the very condition of all virtues, and that abasing themselves, people attain the highest heights, as in glorifying themselves, and they sink to the lowest depths.

Paul encouraged believers to develop the same attitude that Christ had.

Emperor Asoka bowed to Buddhist monk, he said I am doing obeisance to them as a mark of my deep respect for their learning, wisdom and sacrifice. Emperor Asoka also added that matters in life, is not a person's status or position, but his virtues and wisdom.

Rajagopalchari once said, "Man must do his duty and quietly disappear." He also said, "after I pass away none need to remember me."[4] Lala further explain the reasons against humility in leadership:

1. That it interferes with legitimate ambition.

2. That it weakens defence in the righteous cause.

> My dear brothers and sisters, be quick to listen, slow to speak and slow to get angry. (James 1:19)

3. That it diminishes self-confidence.

Leaders need to remember that the Bible shows the power of humility.

Leadership equals humility (Luke 22:24-27). Jesus shows that biblical leadership starts with humility by serving others.

The autocratic, authoritarian leadership style has fallen out of favour among many today. Yet, a subtle, far more powerful approach has appeared, characterized by manipulation and selfish ambition. Making their true intentions, many new-style "leaders" pretend to offer a "win-win" arrangement but they have no real concern for others, except insofar as others can help them achieve their objectives.

Both autocratic and authoritarian styles are out of the question, if we want to lead with Christlikeness. He asks us to take the posture of a servant, to genuinely concern ourselves with the rights, needs, and welfare of those we lead. Christ Himself has provided the example of true servant leadership: not to be served, but to serve and to give.

Power of humility (Matthew 3:11). Often we fail to accept and admit that others are mightier than us? When a person believes strength has the power to dominate, he/she will always be intimidated by those who seem to have more than you – more expertise, more experience, more energy, and more intelligence.

John held a different understanding of strength. He saw it as a gift from God to be used for divine purposes. This gave him tremendous power in his community. His humility gave him the capacity to serve and to welcome others in this case, Jesus –as valuable associates.

Consider Joseph's circumstances, he was in Egypt where people worshiped pagan gods and followed a different culture. Yet, Joseph worshipped the true God. He maintained his faith in such an environment because:

1. He maintained his integrity; he resisted the sexual advances of Potiphar's wife.

2. He kept doing his best even when the situation was the worst, like in prison.

3. He carried out the task he was given, managed famine so well.

4. He used his power and influence compassionately, never took revenge against his enemies such as his brothers, the slave traders and Potiphar's wife.

God used Joseph's faithfulness to fulfil His promise to Abraham. In the same way, God intends to use Christian leaders today in positions, small or big, to accomplish His purpose. Therefore, it is necessary that Christian leaders today honour God through their work, like Joseph.

People are attracted to a leader who is humble and are loyal because they listen, help and uncourageous. If a person desires to have more followers, he/she should begin by being a good friend.

Chapter 8

Compassion, Kindness and Genuine Caring for Others[1]

Compassion is beyond pity.

God is compassionate toward us (Psalm 103-23)

Compassion means sympathetic pity and concern for the suffering or misfortunes of others. Kindness can be defined as the quality of being friendly, generous and considerate. Caring means displaying kindness and concern for others.

A true leader should be genuinely kind, compassionate and loving to earn people's hearts. Leaders can inspire their followers only through love, care, respect than force. People respect how much you care for them not how much you know.

Caring for people is to love, value, appreciate, encourage and reward.

"Well done, good and faithful servant, you have been faithful over a few things, I will make you ruler over many things. Enter into the joy of your lord" (Matthew 25:23)

What is compassion?

Compassion is beyond pity...

> **God's compassion for you is greater than you can imagine!**

Compassion connotes a greater dignity in the object of attention accompanied by an urgent desire to aid.

Compassion is a quality of the heart and of the understanding that makes statesmen rise above their fears, insecurities, reactions and the desire for vengeance.

Every leader should be statesmen. *Statesmanship is defined as, "leadership characterized by wisdom, breadth of vision or regard for general welfare rather than partisan interest."*

The world has witnessed worse situations, millions of innocent are killed. The reason is lack of compassion and selfish interest. Lala[2] describes - in our times Hitler massacred in cold blood six million Jews; the Pol Pot regime in Kampuchea, through killings and privations/lack of food, is estimated to have reduced Kampuchea's populations from six to four million. Add the cost of wars, the purges under Stalin and the killings after the Chinese and Iranian revolutions and we may well ask whether compassion has any place in the governance of nations.

A disciple asked Buddha, "What is the right action?"

"Any action which originates when your mind has compassion" (Dhammapada)

Nehemiah fed hundred and fifty Jews, officials, and others at his table, without any expectation. He, therefore, earned people's favour.

Elisha was kind to the woman who approached him and shared her problem. Elisha showed his compassion and helped the woman through his miracle by filling all her vessels with abundant oil.

Jesus was always aware of the needs of people. *He said Zacchaeus, make haste and come down, for today I must stay at your house* (Luke 19:5). He knew Zacchaeus' need even though there was big crowd around him. In spite of the crowd, He could see Zacchaeus' need.

People don't care how much you know, until you care.

A leader has to have a loving and compassionate heart.

Love is a strong positive emotion of regard and affection.

> **The light of a whole life dies when love is gone.**
> **F. W. Bourdillon**

Lala[3] believes compassion is a deep feeling for and understanding of misery or suffering and the concomitant/ associated desire to promote its alleviation. Compassion is different from pity. Pity suggests condescension (an attitude of patronizing superiority). Compassion connotes a greater dignity in the object of attention accompanied by an urgent desire to aid.

The leader who has love and compassion will have character of generosity. Every Christian leader needs to be generous with time and financial resources. A person can give without loving, but can never love without giving.

"For God so loved the world that he gave his one and only Son, that whoever believes in him shall not perish but have eternal life" (John 3:16).

God's compassion for you is greater than you can imagine.

Christian leaders must set an example through giving, so that everyone in the organization follows them. Generosity is an expression of love of God. Leaders, who are in love with God, will give their time and money to their people. Generosity includes love and compassion.

Joseph forgave his brothers and loved them with gifts and food. He not only saved his people but all of Egypt from starvation. Where there is forgiveness, one can see love and care as a leader.

King David expressed his love and concern even when he was fleeing from Absalom's conspiracy. The king said to Ittai the Gittite, "Why should you come along with us? Go back and stay with king Absalom. And today shall I make you wander about with us, when I do not know where I am going? Go back and take your countrymen. May kindness and faithfulness be with you?" Ittai replied to the king, "As surely as the Lord lives, and as my lord the king lives, wherever my lord the king may be, whether it means life or death, there will your servant be"

What are the lessons? David was kind, sympathetic, loving and caring, even during his troubles. Ittai, was sincere to his master. He could have left the king but he chose to be with him by risking his life and future (2 Samuel 15:19-21).

Nehemiah helps the poor when there was an outcry among his people (Nehemiah 5).

Boaz was kind with his workers and showed compassion to the poor Ruth. A good leader is compassionate to those in need. (Ruth 2).

But the Lord said to Samuel,

> "Do not look at his appearance or at his physical stature, because I have refused him. For the Lord does not see as man sees, for man looks at the outward appearance but the Lord looks at the heart" (1 Samuel 16:7).

God chose David to be king of Israelites because God saw his compassionate heart and tenderness in spirit. David was a warrior but his gentleness was a great character trait. David started his leadership with humility, faithfulness, responsibility, and loves for God and committed his heart to God. Today's leaders need to emulate David as they climb the ladder of leadership.

When Jerusalem fell to King Nebuchadnezzar in 587 BC, the Babylonians burnt down the royal palace and Nebuchadnezzar had the King of Judah blinded. Almost fifty years later Cyrus, founder of the Persian Empire, is believed to have received a revelation from the Lord of Israel "to rebuild my city Jerusalem and set my people free." When Cyrus conquered Babylon he liberated the Jews and directed them to go and rebuild Jerusalem. In the age of religious intolerance, Cyrus demonstrated remarkable tolerance; in an age of cruelty he showed magnanimity as well as concern[4] (read more Lala p.31).

Chapter 9

A Genuine Desire to Serve Others, Putting Service Ahead of Self-Interest[1]

Each of you should look not only to your own interests,
but also to the interests of others. Philippians 2:4
God's power working within you can help you to resist your selfish desires.
No greedy leaders! "...*not given to drunkenness, not violent but gentle, not*
quarrelsome, not a lover of money" 1 Timothy 3:3

A true leader has to be a servant first from his/her heart and mind.
The success of a leader depends upon the success and
satisfaction of people whom he/she serves. Serving and
honouring is the greatest honour and obligation of a servant leader.
People's interest should be ahead of self.

Leaders are called to give up their rights, if they have desire to serve
others and put service ahead of self-interest. *People's rights are leader's*
duty. Whenever, leaders fight for their rights, they will face frustration,
disappointment and even get angry. This can be called negative
approach or mind-set of a leader. When leaders forget their rights,

they will have full energy, commitment and can achieve their goals or responsibilities.

Leaders are supposed to add value to others by compassion and care. Their success depends on how much they care and help. ZigZigler says,

Start focusing on people rather than yourself to add value to others.

John Maxwell suggests three steps – putting others first in your thinking, finding out what others need and meeting that need with excellence and generosity.

> **Ask God to give you strength and energy to help others-he promises to provide all that you need.**

He further calls to invest in empowering others. Empowering people takes a personal investment, it requires time and energy. But it is worth the price. If you do it right, you will have the privilege of seeing someone move up to a higher level. And when you empower others, you create power in your organization.

In Christian realm all leadership should be servant leadership. Servant leadership is best defined by Jesus Himself when He said, "Whoever wants to become great among you must be your servant and whoever wants to be first must be your slave- just as the Son of Man did not came to be served but to serve and give his life as a ransom for many." In God's Kingdom, true power to influence comes as we serve.

Try to forget yourself in the service of others. God's power working within can help to resist selfish desires and promote to serve others better. For when a person think too much of themselves and their own interests, they really become despondent. But when they work for others, efforts return to bless us. (Sidney Powell).

In servant leader one should.[2]

1. Have sense of call

2. Put others ahead of their own agenda

3. Possess confidence to serve

4. Initiate service to others

5. Not position conscious

6. Serve out of love

> People are attracted to a person who is loyal, who listens, who helps, and who encourages. If you desire more friends, begin by being good friend to others.

The fact that Joshua was prepared for the responsibilities of leadership, is evidenced by by his unswerving loyalty and devotion. He is called the servant of Moses.

In Christian leadership, motives are as crucial as the actual work. "Be shepherds of God's flock that is under your care, serving as overseers – not because you must but because you are willing, as God wants you to be; not greedy for money but eager to serve; not lording it over those entrusted to you, but being examples to the flock."[3]

The proper understanding of servant leadership of authority is essential to Christian leadership. Scripture teaches four major principles of authority:[4]

1. God establishes authority, beginning in the home, then in the church, the government and at work and school.

2. God expects submission to authority, respecting those over you and willingly supporting their leadership.

3. God enables a person to submit to authority, receiving correction, admitting mistakes, being accountable, and showing true loyalty and respect.

4. God exemplifies submission to authority. Jesus the Son submitted to the Father, even to His death on the cross.

The apostle Paul called on his disciples 'to follow me as I follow Christ.' In their submission, Jesus and Paul provide the perfect model for all Christian leaders.

To serve others ahead of self-demands power of self-sacrifice. What does power look like in the lives of people you know? Does it mean aggressively making things happen? Does it mean political or financial muscle? Jesus described His power as the right and ability to lay down His life for others.

For whom or what would you lay down your life? Is there a cause so noble or people so dear that you would willingly let go of life itself? The world may not view that kind of self-sacrifice as power. But we who follow Christ can know the profound power of love-looking out not only for our own interest, but also for the interest of others.

Chapter 10

Tough Minded Optimism

*T*he quality of a successful leader is optimism, clear and tough mind. Optimism means hopefulness and confidence about future or success. Optimism can bring enthusiasm, excitement and strength even in difficult times. Without enthusiasm nothing great can be achieved. Tough-minded optimism helps leaders face stress and become tough mentally.

As a leader one should be an optimistic person. An optimistic leader will naturally seek to see the good in the future and bring the team to create positive change together.

Leaders can be tough and tender hearted. Leaders can be tough and optimistic. Such leaders are always willing to face problems, and look for solutions. They find innovative methods to solve problems. Sometimes they are forced to take tough decisions with optimistic approach. Tough minded leaders never stop till they reach a solution.

Optimism in leadership means looking at the bright side of life. Optimistic leader are excited about the future and there is certain energy in their life. Optimism gives energy and pessimism drains energy.

Abraham took a tough and painful decision in sending Hagar away.

Abraham decided to offer his son Isaac to God, an act of faith, and an extremely tough decision. Abraham did not withhold his only son. He knew that God was testing his heart not Isaac's life. Abraham's life exemplifies a tough mind and an optimistic attitude for leaders today.

Hannah is a woman who personifies ideal motherhood. Hannah longed for a son out of her own womb to love and fondle. God gave her a son (Samuel) after hearing her prayer and commitment. Hannah made tough decision and gave Samuel to the Lord. God rewarded Hannah with five children because of her faith and sacrifice. When leaders take tough decisions, they have to pay a price. Of course they will be blessed.

Ruth, Moabite widow, went with her mother-in-law Naomi, leaving her people and land. By any yardstick it was a tough decision. It is difficult to say whether her decision was based on optimism, but the decision was undoubtedly based on her compassion and love towards Naomi. God showed favour by providing Boaz as husband.

Chapter 11

Self-Awareness

*S*elf-awareness *means to have knowledge or perception of a situation or fact of self.* Apart from having core values such as integrity and trust, self-awareness is crucial. *Self-awareness includes self-knowledge and self-confidence.* Having self-knowledge means possessing clear, intimate understanding and insight into:

1. Who you are and what and why you think and feel?

2. What you do and how do it?

A leader's self-awareness is crucial. This demands seeing self properly. When one views himself/herself according to the Word of God, they will begin to have a proper view of their potential. Jon Byler mentions three "truth declarations" that will help individuals see themselves properly.[1]

1. I am uniquely created by God

2. God has a plan for my life

3. I can develop my God-given potential

> *For jealousy and selfishness is not God's kind of wisdom. Such things are earthly, unspiritual and motivated by the Devil. For wherever there is jealously and selfish ambition, there you will find disorder and every kind of evil. (James 3:15-16)*

Self-awareness examines and assesses your values, beliefs, strengths, limitations, natural tendencies, biases, weaknesses, motivations, feeling, habits and behaviour.

God chose Moses and David because they had all the qualities of a true leader, and were aware of who they were, what they were doing and understood God's vision.

When a leader is assertive, intelligent, courageous, he/ she can be called strong. When leaders are positive, inspiring, enthusiastic, passionate, genuine, energetic, and constantly working towards empowering and developing his/her followers, they are transformational leaders. Every leader has to improve leadership skills. Kendra Cherry suggests following tips to become better leaders:

1. Learn more about your leadership styles

2. Encourage creativity

3. Serve as a role model

4. Be passionate and enthusiastic for work they have taken up

5. Listen and communicate effectively

6. Have a positive attitude

7. Encourage people to involve, participate and make them contribute to the organization positively

8. Motivate your followers

9. Offer rewards and recognition

10. Keep trying new things

PART 2

Christian Leadership Role

Chapter 12

Christian Leadership[1]

Let each man find out what God wants him to do,
And then let him do it, or die in the attempt. Charles Spurgeon

Christian Leadership

*W*ho is a leader? According to the Webster on-line dictionary *a leader is one who directs on a course of action or in a direction.* In layman's terms, *a leader is someone who has the courage to lead and the humility to help others lead.* Who is a Christian? According to the Webster on-line dictionary *a Christian is one who professes belief in the teachings of Jesus Christ.*

A Christian leader is one who inspires others to live in a Christ-like manner, and lives with integrity. This is essential role of a Christian leader. A Christian leader is not only *"One who directs another to believe in the teachings of Jesus Christ"* but also sets an example and inspires others to live as we do. A Christian leader helps others in need, shows their passion and love for the Lord, and is humble in all things. A Christian leader does not have to be a pastor, deacon, or elder of the church. Look right next to you and you may see a dedicated choir member, an ambitious young adult, or a child memorizing a Bible verse, and these are the Christian leaders. Just by being a Christian you are already a leader. A Christian leader will face three questions, what do leaders dream about? Are they passionate? If yes, what are they passionate about? And what will bring joy?

A basic description of leadership is the duty and call of the person who is in charge to take charge with courage and character, and to risk leading his/her people where they need to go and how they need to be led. It is a position that seeks vision, opportunities, and needs, and then motivates others to get it done through the resources, talents and time they can contribute.

Every Christian leader need to remember to learn, and grow in Christ before they lead others. To manage a church effectively, leaders must seriously take their lead from scriptural principles and not from secular trends. During the times of trouble, turn to God and wait patiently for His help. He will never fail you. One will enjoy great comfort and joy, if they understand that God is rich in grace and mercy. As David prays:

> You alone are my strength, my Shield,
> To you alone may my spirit yield?
> You alone are my heart's desire.
> And I long to worship you.

God is the ultimate leader and He calls every believer to lead others. God chose His own creation, human beings to lead, and not any animal because humans possess spirit and capacities to relate to Him and follow Him. When humans fell into sin, God could have changed His plan by finishing Adam and Eve. But yet, He called us to follow Him and lead others.

Every time God desired to do something great, He called leaders and even with no leadership qualities to complete His plan, God used Abraham to raise nation, Moses to deliver His people from Egypt and Joshua to lead His people to Promised Land. Today, He calls every Christian for the great task to strengthen His plan both large and small. Are you ready for the role God wants from you?

> *"You yourself must be an example to them by doing good deeds of every kind. Let everything you do reflect the integrity and seriousness of your teaching. Let your teaching be so correct that it can't be criticized. Then those who want to argue will be ashamed because they won't have anything bad to say about us.... You must teach these things and encourage your people to do them, correcting them which necessary. You have the authority to do this, so don't let anyone ignore you or disregard what you say" (Titus 2:7-8, 15).*

If you want to become a leader, asks God to develop these traits in you - honesty, kindness, patience, purity and integrity.

Christian leaders have a wider role to play than secular leaders. Their role is vital for their family, church, work place, society etc.

Remember in Christian leadership "excellence starts at the top." Moses set an excellent example for his work force, while he constructed the tabernacle (Exodus 40:16). Can Christian leaders follow Moses model of excellence and quality at their work place?

If person is faithful in the small things, God will trust him/her with greater responsibilities, like leaders in the Bible.

In part II, I would like to deal with Christian leader's responsibilities/role as shepherd, as servant, as spiritual leader, a facilitator's role, as biblical leader, role in church, role with youth ministry, role as transparent leader etc.

Chapter 13

Christian Leader's Role as a shepherd[1]

The Lord as the Shepherd of His People "The Lord is my shepherd, I shall not want." (Psalms 23:1)

With upright heart he shepherded them and guided them with his skilful hand. Psalm 78:72

Shepherd leadership is the leadership of a shepherd.

What is Christian leadership? What should a Christian leader be like? There is no fine example for Christian leadership than our Lord Jesus Christ. Leaders with a heart for people are called shepherd leaders. The role of a Christian leader is beautifully dealt by Got Questions Ministries, and compared to a Shepherd's role like Jesus Christ. There is no finer example for Christian leadership than our Lord Jesus Christ. Jesus is the Good Shepherd. He declared,

"I am the good shepherd".

The good shepherd lays down his life for the sheep.

"The hired hand is not the shepherd who owns the sheep" (John 10:11).

It is within this verse that we see the perfect description of a Christian leader. A Christian leader is one who acts as a shepherd to those "sheep" in his/her care. Let me highlight the role of a Christian leader to that of a shepherd. The shepherd is one who has several roles in regard to his/her sheep.

1. A shepherd leads, feeds, nurtures, comforts, corrects and protects.

2. A Christian leader is one who follows Christ and inspires others to follow Him as well.

3. A Christian leader also comforts the sheep, binding up their wounds and apply the balm of compassion and love

4. A Christian leader also feeds and nourishes the sheep, and the ultimate "sheep food" is the word of God

5. Just as a shepherd uses a crook to pull a wandering sheep back into the fold, Christian leader corrects and disciplines those in his/her care when they go astray

6. The final role of a Christian leader is that of a protector.

Psalms 23 describes the functions of a shepherd leader and God's nature, and also about His leadership.

> "The Lord is my shepherd; I shall not want. He makes me to lie down in green pastures; He leads me beside the still waters. He restores my soul; He leads me in the paths of righteousness for His name's sake. Yea, though I walk through the valley of the shadow of death, I will fear no evil. For you are with me; your rod and your staff, they comfort me. You prepare a table before me in the presence of enemies; you anoint my head with oil, my cup runs over. Surely goodness and mercy shall follow me All the days of my life; and I will dwell in the house of the Lord forever" (Psalms 23: 1-6)

The word 'Shepherd' communicates the love, nurture and spiritual care that a godly leader provides. A good shepherd.[2]

•   Provides necessities
•   Confidently leads

- Guides and directs
- Feeds and anoints
- Loves unconditionally
- Gives rest
- Renews and restores
- Protects from harm
- Corrects and comforts
- Furnishes permanent shelter

> *I am the good shepherd. The good shepherd lays down his life for th e sheep. John 10:11*

The Bible is the best source which describes the work of the shepherd:

1. To be gentle and tender
2. To guide and lead
3. To watch
4. To feed
5. To restore and heal

> *We belong to the Lord, the Good shepherd. (Psalm 23:1-6)*

Peter Nsowah says that it is not only Jesus who is described as shepherd, but Jehovah describes Himself as a shepherd. All through in the Old Testament, Jehovah describes Himself as the shepherd who works hard to take care of His sheep. What better example could we learn from the example of Jehovah Himself? We can look at some of the key activities that Almighty God Himself undertakes as He demonstrates the true functions of a shepherd (Read Ezekiel 34).

God wants Christian leaders to be humble, loving. Church leadership is ministry, not management.

> Leaders in the church are called as shepherds. This requires involvement in a personal shepherding ministry among the people. The shepherd leader unpacks the four primary ministries of shepherds-knowing, feeding, leading and protecting on macro (church wide) and micro (personal) levels, providing seven elements to incorporate into an effective shepherding plan (Sinclair Ferguson).

Shepherds were expected to be faithful and diligent, so much so that their occupation was often used as a metaphor for spiritual defection and leadership, either positively or negatively. Sheep came to know their shepherds voice so well that they would follow only them. Shepherds provided water and food for their flocks and when an animal was lost, they were expected to go out and find it. Shepherd also protected their flocks, risking their lives if necessary.

In the Old Testament, God is often called a Shepherd. He protects and seeks out His flock, Israel. Likewise in the New Testament, Jesus refers to Himself as the Good Shepherd who cares for, protects and redeems His people. He even suffers for the sheep and separates them from the goats on the day of judgement. As the Great Shepherd of the sheep, Jesus calls spiritual leaders to be under shepherds.[3]

Those who God designates as leaders are called not to be governing monarchs, but humble slaves, not slick celebrities but labouring servants. Those who would lead God's people must above all exemplify sacrifice, devotion, submission and lowliness. Jesus Himself gave in the pattern when He stooped to wash His disciples' feet, a task customarily done by the lowest of slaves. If the Lord of the universe would do that, no church leader has a right to think of himself as a bigwig.

The primary biblical image of servant leadership is that of a shepherd, because the flock is not there for the sake of the shepherd; the shepherd is there for the sake of the flock (Ken Blanchard).

Chapter 14

Servant Leadership[1]

Instead whoever wants to become great among? you must be your servant, and whoever wants to be first must be your slave-just as the Son of Man did not come to be served, but to serve, and to give his life as a ransom for many.
(Matthew 20:26-28)

When he had finished washing their feet, he put on his clothes and returned to his place. "Do you understand? what I have done for you?" he asked them, "You call me 'Teacher' and 'Lord,' and rightly so, for that is what I am. Now that I, your Lord and Teacher, have washed your feet, you also should wash one another's feet. I have set you an example that you should do as I have done for you. (John 13:12-15)

Who is a servant leader?

A *servant leader is someone who is servant first,* who has responsibility to be in the world and so he/she contributes to the well-being of people and community. A servant looks to the needs of the people and asks them how he/she can help them to solve problems and promote personal development. Servant leaders place their main focus on people, because only content and motivated people are able to reach their targets and to fulfil the set expectations. Servant leaders are people who first wants to serve and not be served. In spiritual leadership, God's touch in leadership should be seen. Without God's touch, leader's words, actions or even motivational seminars, looks like class room teaching.

Jesus Himself best defined servant leadership in the following passage:

> *"Whoever wants to become great among you must be your servant, and whoever wants to be first must be your slave – just as the Son of Man did not come to be served, but to serve, and to give his life as a ransom for many."(Matthew 20:26-28)*Jesus modelled the true servant style of leadership. He, the Lord incarnate, bent down and washed their feet, teaching them the true measures of leading by first serving others (John 13:12-17). The term servant speaks of low power, low prestige, low respect and low honour. Most people are not attracted for low-value and low profile jobs.

When Jesus washed his disciple's feet, He demonstrated a fundamental principle that He regularly stressed to His followers. *To lead others, one must serve others.* This is as true in public life and the business world or in churches. Leaders, therefore, are expected to be consistent, and to have a clear attitude of a servant placing others' needs before one's own. They also have to commit to do concrete things to meet those needs and not look for favours or reciprocity from the people they serve.

Jesus' promise (John 14:12-13) shows that noble leadership seeks to empower others to achieve results even greater than the leader has achieved. A true leader seeks to achieve great goals more than great personal gain. Rather than being intimidated by his/her followers' potential, they rejoice in their growth, development and achievements.

Responding to a controversy among the disciples, Jesus revealed a unique style of authority-servant leadership. What does it mean to be a "slave" in order to become great? What does it mean to define leadership in terms of servant hood? Jesus suggested that both involve seeking the highest good for others good as evaluated from God's perspective.

In the light of Jesus' own example particularly in giving up His own life as a "ransom for many" – we can observe that servant leadership means (Matthew 25:28):

1. Seeing ourselves as called by God to serve or lead others

2. Knowing intimately the people we serve or lead

3. Caring deeply about the people we serve or lead

4. Being willing to sacrifice our own convenience to meet the needs of the people we serve or lead

Servant leadership is both a leadership philosophy and set of leadership practices. Servant leadership includes both individual and organization, which have faith and bring a change. There are many who want to exercise authority but few who are willing to take the towel and basin and wash feet. Paul reminds us that our attitude is to be like Christ's, in that we consider others better than ourselves and do nothing out of selfishness; rather we look out for the interests of others. From biblical perspective, servant leadership is not only being free of abuse of power but is first and foremost based on mutual respect and love for one another. *In Christianity all leadership should be servant leadership.*

In the words of Robert K. Grendeaf, servant leadership can be defined:

> "The servant leadership is servant first…It begins with the natural feeling that one wants to serve first. Then conscious choice brings one to aspire to lead. That person is sharply different from one who is leader first, perhaps because of the need to assuage an unusual power drive or to acquire material possessions… The leader-first and the servant first are two extreme types. Between them there are shadings and blends that are part of the infinite variety of human nature." "The difference manifests itself in the

care taken by the servant-first to make sure that other people's highest priority needs are being served. The best test, and difficult to administer is: Do those served grow as persons? Do they, while being served, become healthier, wiser, freer, more autonomous, more likely themselves to become servants? And, what is the effect on the least privileged in society? Will they benefit or at least not be further deprived?"

John Mott captured well the heart of spiritual leadership as follows, *"Leadership in the sense of rendering service, leadership in the sense of the largest unselfishness, in the sense of full hearted absorption in the greatest work of the world, building up the kingdom of our Lord Jesus Christ"*

The concept servant leadership is mentioned in ancient and religious texts. In Christianity, the passage from the Gospel of Mark is often mentioned of servant leadership.

"But Jesus called them (his disciples) to Himself and said to them,

"You know that those who are considered rulers over the Gentiles, lord it over them and their great ones exercise authority over them. Yet it shall not be so among you; but whoever desires to become great among you shall be your servant. And whoever of you desires to be first shall be slave of all. For even the son of Man did not come to be served, but to serve, and to give His life a ransom for many" (Mark 10:42-45).

> Ask God to give you strength and energy to help others – he promises to provide all that you need.

Islam believes *"the leader of a people is their servant."*

Chanaky wrote in his book Arthashastra.

"The king (leader) shall consider as good, not what pleases himself but what pleases his subjects (followers), the king is a paid servant and enjoys the resources of the state together with people"

The Chinese sage Lao Tzu wrote The Tao TeChing, a simple treatise on servant leadership as:

The great leader forgets her/him and attends to the development of others.

Good leaders support the bottom ten per cent.

Great leader know that the diamond in the rough   Is always found in the rough.

In most cultures it is emphasized in history, holistic, co-operative, communal, intuitive, and caring and spiritual values in servant leadership.

The leadership in the context of servant leadership can be three styles of leadership – autocratic, participative and Laissez-faire.

Servant leadership can be associated with participative leadership style. The authoritarian style will not be in harmony with servant leadership style. The priority of servant leadership is to encourage, support and enable subordinates to unfold their full potential and abilities. It is, therefore, in servant leadership that there is more scope for delegation of responsibilities and participative decision making. If you wish to be a leader you will be frustrated, for very few people wish to be led. If you aim to be a servant you will never be frustrated.

Servant leaders desire to invest in others to see the vision accomplished. Jesus' hope was for His followers to do "great things," even more than He had accomplished (John 14:12). Moreover, the time frame of His vision was the future; it was only after His ascension that His followers "turned the world upside down" (Acts 17:6). Thus, He was not merely doing things for His own accomplishment for the present. He built others for their accomplishments to the future.[2]

Servant hood is not about position or skill of a leader, but it is about attitude. The truth is that the best leaders serve others before they serve themselves. According to John Maxwell, true servant leaders are those who:

- Put others ahead of their own agenda
- Possess the confidence to serve
- Initiate service to others
- Are not position-conscious
- Serve out of love.

Leaders need to know that their influence has less to do with position or title than it does with life's attitude. More than position, the leadership result and credibility are vital. Leaders gain credibility when their actions speak and when they add value to others.

> *I command you to love each other in the same way that I love you. And here is how to measure it- the greatest love is shown when people lay down their lives for their friends. (John 15:12-13)*

A servant leader has to have high degree of credibility. King David no doubt a great leader but he lost his credibility, when he turned to married woman and killed her husband. David was in habit of picking and choosing when he would listen to God. King Solomon also lost his leadership credibility, when he did not listen to God and the counsel of his advisors and took many wives and allowed them to worship other gods.

Chapter 15

Characteristics of Servant Leadership[1]

A humble act of sacrifice proves greatness. Mark 14:1-9

Most scholars agree that servant leaders need to have the following characteristics to serve as a servant. Robert K. Grenleaf who is recognized as the father of servant leadership mentions the following characteristics of servant leadership:

1. Listening

A wise man will hear and increase learning (Proverbs 1:1).

The moment you stop learning you stop leading (Rick Warren).

In servant leadership, a manger or leadership is required to have communication skills as well as the competence to make decisions. A servant leader has the motivation to listen actively to subordinates and support them in decision identification. A servant leader particularly needs to pay attention to what remains unspoken in the management setting. This means relying on his/her inner voice in order to find out what the body, mind and spirit communicate.

Noah's life is a great example of obedience and faith in God. He quietly listened to God to build a boat in spite of people ridiculing him. Noah's life revealed qualities of patience, persistence and that of an obedient listener, God blessed and saved Noah, just as he will faithfully bless and protect those who follow and obey Him even today.

> *"Listen now to my voice, I will give you counsel and will be with you"* (Exodus 18:19).

A good leader is a good listener and communicator, who should be consistent, clear, and courteous. If leaders are not good listeners then ....

- They stop gaining wisdom
- They stop hearing what is being said
- Team members stop communicating
- Their indifference begins to spread to other area

Finally, poor listening leads to hostility, miscommunication and breakdown of team cohesion.[1]

2. *Empathy*

A servant leader attempts to understand and empathize with others. Workers may be considered not only as employees, but also as people who need respect and appreciation of their personal development. As a result, leadership is seen as a special type of human work, which ultimately generates a competitive advantage.

At one stage, Moses was weary of complaints, stagnation and lack of progress among the people. In this weakened condition he made hasty decisions that cost him his future. God told him to speak to a rock in order to get water but in anger, he struck it. He reacted in fury rather than obeying with poise, and for this disobedience he was not allowed to enter the Promised Land. This sad incident teaches two lessons. First, never make a major decision during an emotionally low time. Second, choose to be proactive, not reactive in your leadership.[2]

3. Healing

A great strength of a servant leader is the ability for healing one's self and others. A servant leader tries to help people solve their problems and conflicts in relationships, because he/she wants to encourage and support the personal development of each individual. This leads to the formation of a business culture, in which the working environment is dynamic, fun and free of fear of failure.

4. Awareness

A servant leader needs to gain general awareness and specially self-awareness. He/she has to have ability to view situations from a more integrated, holistic position. As a result, a servant leader gets a better understanding about ethics and values.

5. Persuasion

A servant leader does not take advantage of their power and status by coercing compliance; they rather try to convince those they manage. This element distinguishes servant leadership most clearly from tradition, authoritarian models and can be traced back to the religious views.

Moses and Joshua were great example of persuasion, in spite of that their people were most unhappy and disgruntle. Both persuaded the people to believe God's promise and Joshua led them to the Promised Land. Persuasion works even without power if a leader has clear vision and commitment.

Perseverance is the act or state of persisting in anything undertaken, continued pursuit or prosecution of any business, plan or effort.

Let us not become weary in doing good, for at the proper time we will reap a harvest if we do not give up (Galatians 6:9).

Be on your guard; stand firm in the faith; be men of courage; be strong (1 Corinthians 16:13).

Jacob wrestled with the angel all night and he did not give up. He was determined to hold on till the end, until he received the blessings he was looking for.

6.   *Conceptualization*

A servant leader thinks beyond day-to-day realities. That means he/she has the ability to see beyond the limits of the operating business and also focuses on long term operating goals. A leader constructs a personal vision that only he/she can develop by reflecting on the meaning of life. As a result, he derives specific goals and implementation strategies.

We have great leaders in the Bible, who exhibited this quality of conceptualization or thought beyond day-to-day events and realities,

7.   *Foresight*

Foresight is the ability to foresee the likely outcome of a situation. It enables the servant leader to learn about the past and to achieve a better understanding about the current reality. It also enables the servant leader to identify consequences about the future. This characteristic is closely related to conceptualization.

Leaders will have clear foresight if they have faith in God like Abraham. Abraham underwent the biggest testing of his when God asked him to sacrifice Isaac, the only son of Abraham. Abraham obeyed, fully prepared to slay his son, while fully trusting God and foreseeing God's plan, to either resurrect Isaac from the dead or provide substitute sacrifice.

8. *Stewardship*

Stewards like overseers, were entrusted with responsibility for their superiors. In the New Testament, a steward is sometimes referred to as a guardian or curator or as a manager or household superintendent. Paul called himself a "steward" of Christ's household, responsible to Christ for carrying out his task of preaching the gospel to the Gentiles. *All Christians have been given resources and responsibilities by God and are accountable to Him for their stewardship over those gifts.*

In Scripture and theology, a minister of Christ/church leader, whose duty is to dispense the provisions of the gospel, to preach its doctrines and administer its ordinances is stewardship. It is required in stewardship that a person is found faithful (1 Corinthians 4). Leader or a trustee will have the task to hold their church in trust for the greater good of society. Servant leadership is seen as an obligation to help and serve others. Openness and persuasion are more important than control.

> "Needless to say, you can love people without leading them, but you cannot lead people without loving them" (John Maxwell).

Moses and Joshua are great example of stewardship. They were open yet were task masters to fulfil God's mission.

9. *Commitment to the growth of people*

Servant leaders are convinced that people have intrinsic value beyond their contributions as workers/church members. Therefore, they should nurture the personal, professional and spiritual growth of people, not self. Leaders must be close enough to relate to others, but far enough ahead to motivate (John Maxwell). The growth of leadership and church depends on the people or church members

Joseph trusted God no matter how bad a situation he was in. He saved not only his own people but all of Egypt from starvation. Here, Joseph was committed for the wellbeing of his people and also people of Egypt.

Moses helped people of Hebrew from slavery in Egypt to the land of Canaan. Moses was committed to his people's freedom and development. Finally, Joshua also had the same commitment and he fulfilled Moses and God's plan. Both lived with the people to know their problems and faith, confidence, and followed God in order to solve people's problems.

10. Building community

A servant leader builds a strong community within his organization and wants a true community in the institutions/church. Building a Christian community is equally important as that of a church. The strength of leadership depends not only on the strength of the church but the community as a whole. Therefore, servant leadership instead building themselves and church, need to build a strong community first. It is crucial to create an environment which will be in harmony with growth of an organization. When an organization grows, it is never easy, but a good environment makes swim upstream easy. A good environment means an atmosphere where there are challenges challenge with forward focus, a willingness to change, and allows others to grow and a leader who can be a model for the team.

Joshua, a faithful and obedient servant of God, led his people to Canaan, won the battle and built communities (12 communities).

Leaders take time to build communities. Great example can be how Moses trained Joshua. Moses passed along his authority, abilities and anointing to Joshua. He gave Joshua his time, his insight, a learning environment, an opportunity to prove himself and a strong belief in his future. Moses and Joshua's relation demonstrates that producing a leader is not a quick, simple process but it requires time, emotional investment and sacrifice.

When a leader wishes to develop future leaders, recognize that followers will need conviction, courage, obedience, and equipping from their leader, and vision from God and acceptance from people. With time, investment and sacrifice, will build a legacy of leadership. God takes time to prepare leaders for a particular purpose. The purpose is more important than the waiting period.

God prepared Moses not in a day, but over time, not through an event, but with process. Moses spent his first forty years in the desert before God called him to lead the Hebrews out of Egypt. As per John Maxwell, God also lead others through a lengthy leadership development process:

- *Noah waited 120 years before the predicted rains arrived.*

- *Abraham waited 120 years for the promised son*

- *Job waited perhaps a lifetime, 60-70 years, for God's justice*

Larry Spears has identified ten characteristics that help to convey the power of servant leadership concept:

1. Servant leaders have a sharp level of general awareness, but even sharper awareness of themselves.

2. Servant leaders see themselves as stewards that hold resources in trust for another

3. Servant leaders listen intently to the needs expressed by their co-workers, employees, and communities.

4. Servant leaders strive to empathize with others by listening receptively and openly.

5. Servant leaders have foresight, the ability to foresee the likely outcome of situation.

6. Servant leaders see a balance between conceptualization, dreaming great dream and the need to operationalize day-to-day functions.

7. Servant leaders rely less on authority and more on the use of moral persuasion as a basis of influence.

8. Servant leaders are committed to the growth of people in all circumstances

9. Servant leaders are community builders.

Christ teaches harmonious community, love, humility and servant hood. Alexander Strauch, suggests master's teaching like gentleness, humble, servants of all, sacrifice, service and suffering, humble shall be exalted, one who serves and washing one another's feet are important.

To build a child, the involvement of community is essential. Similarly, the community or church is needed to build a leader. Leaders are not built automatically. It is the responsibility of entire church to build next generation of leader. There is leadership crisis in churches around the world, mainly in India. 90% feel pastors are inadequately trained to cope with ministry demands and 50% feel unable to meet the needs of the job.[3] Let us remember that healthy leaders are built in a community/church and healthy leaders can lead healthy community/church.

Chapter 16

Servant Leadership Keys[1]

Instead, whoever wants to become great among you? must be your servant, and whoever wants to be first must be your slave – just as the Son of Man did not come be served, but to serve, and to give his life as a ransom for many (Matthew 20:26-28).

Servant leadership keys as per Don Page:

1. Purpose

The mission of the organization must have a larger purpose – something beyond producing goods or services. Employees want to feel instinctively that their work is making a positive difference. A servant leader's primary objective is to serve others. Servant-leader seeks to serve the well-being of others through their goals and work, through which they make a positive difference in society.

The very essence of leadership is its purpose. And the purpose of leadership is to accomplish a task. That is what leadership does and what it does is more important than what it is or how it works (Colonel Dandridge M. Malone).

Paul had great purpose, to preach and build churches.

After Paul had seen the vision (purpose), we got ready at once to leave for Macedonia, concluding that God had called us to preach the gospel to them (Acts 16:10)

2. Ownership

Employees want to review themselves as having a part in shaping how their work is to be done. In servant-led organizations, employees want to be consulted and included in decision making as partners in the enterprise.

Once Nehemiah invited, consulted and shared the purpose of building the wall of Jerusalem, people responded by saying, *"Let us start rebuilding, so they began this good work."* Even today, leaders need to take the people into confidence and allow them to be part of great work and own the achievement. If they fail to join, they will lose share in the great work like Sanballat the Horonite, Tobiah the Ammonite official and Geshem and Arab lost being part of great work (Nehemiah 2:17-20).

3. Oneness

When there is a prevailing sense that we are all in this together," working relations become more collaborative. Servant leadership is based on team work in which contributing to the collective effort rather than position is important.

Joshua showed his team building quality during the fall of Jericho. Israelites showed that they are together.

> *"When the trumpets sounded, the people shouted, and at the sound of the trumpet, when the people gave a loud shout, the wall collapsed, to every man charged straight in, in and they took the city. They devoted the city to the Lord and destroyed with the sword every living in it – men and women, young and old, cattle, sheep and donkeys"* (Joshua 6: 20-21)

4. Relationship Building

The workplace should offer ways to build healthy interpersonal relationships that foster loyalty to the institution and its team members in promoting their collective efforts. Servant leadership is based on collective teamwork and is often referred to as relational leadership. Community building is integral to servant leadership being successful. Leadership required followers and that leads in inter-personal relationships being built.

5. Service

Employees enjoy learning from and helping one another. This can be fostered through formal mentoring or training programs or more informal on the spot coaching or assisting with project. Servant leaders are committed to equipping and investing in the lives of their employees so that these employees can advance to their full potential.

6. Equality

All people in the organization are considered to be equally important regardless of their position and treated as such. In servant leadership, responsibilities are more important than the perks of position entitlement. The servant leader is first among equals.

7. Validation

Employees can see for themselves the impact of their work and be affirmed for it. The servant-leader encourages input and feedback and shares credit for the results.

8. Invention

Risk taking in the name of innovation is encouraged and failures are the price of learning rather than the reason for dismissal. The servant leader welcomes open discussion on means for improvement and learning from one's mistakes.

9. Personal development

People are able to reach their full potential through learning and expanded job opportunities. Taking people to a higher level is at the heart of servant leadership.

10. Acknowledgement

Employers are recognized for their efforts and successes through genuine appreciation. Praise is generously given to others for their accomplishments. The servant leader focuses on the "we" and the "I" of who gets credit for what.

11. Balance

Employers respect the fact that there's life beyond work when making assignments. The service ethic is an attitude that prevails and must be given expression in all of one's life and not just on the job.

12. Challenge

The work place is seen as an opportunity to take on challenges for those who want them. Serving others has no limits so there are always new opportunities to serve others in meeting their needs, many of which will be unexpected, thereby creating a challenge for those who respond.

13. Dialogue

There is on-going, honest, and constructive dialogue involving people at all levels of the organization as well as significant suppliers and customers. Information is to be shared, and listening receptively is a distinctive feature of servant leadership. The servant leader seeks first to understand and then to be understood.

14. Direction

There is a compelling vision that draws people into a common direction. Organizational visions and mission are arrived at through discussions so that all members are on board with the direction to be taken.

15. Flexibility

Good judgment is used in applying rules. Values are more important than rules in motivating employees in the right direction because values are rooted in meaning. Many will fail at life if they are unwilling to change.

16. Informality

An open door policy is practiced by everyone and protocol is not seen as a stumbling block. Servant leaders are regularly seen interacting with others and maintain an open-door atmosphere for development and encouraging each other. In serving, there is no hierarchy that impedes communication in all directions.

17. Relevance

Red tape does not take people away from engaging in relevant activities. Servant leaders build on trust and values more than protocol to reach their goals. There is always an unselfish motive involved in servant leadership.

18. Respect

Employees show respect for one another regardless of their rank or title. Authority is based on influence from within through encouragement, inspiration, motivation and persuasion that are rooted in respect for the other person being served.

19. Self - identity

Individuality is encouraged and the organization respects the need of people to have their own space in which to work. One can only serve together out of a healthy self-respect. Respect for the person and their diversity is at the heart of understanding whom one serves.

20. Support

Employees are given resources like information, time, funding, experience, learning, opportunity, tools etc. which they need to succeed in their work. The task of the servant leader is to provide all the means whereby others can reach their options through on-going development of the collective mission.

21. Worth

Employees are genuinely valued and their interests are taken into account when decisions are made. Decisions are collectively arrived at. The antithesis of servant leadership is self-seeking top-down leadership. Acceptance and empathy are at the core of servant leadership.

Servant leader lose the right to be selfish. Servant leader has to gain servant heart.

We who are strong ought to bear with the failings of the weak and not to please ourselves. Each of us should please his neighbour for his good, to build him up. For even Christ did not please himself but, as it is written: "The insults of those who insult you have fallen on me". For everything that was written in the past was written to teach us, so that through endurance and the encouragement of the Scriptures we might have hoped (Romans 15:1-6).

1. A servant leadership is to serve others not wielding to self
2. A servant leader declines self and serve others
3. A servant leader first develops others before self and values others life
4. A servant leader forgive those who mistreat him
5. A servant leader remains to be student and always willing to learn
6. A servant leader always pursue harmonious relationship, unity and peace
7. A servant leader imitates Christ and follows Jesus as a model.

Anyone can follow a path, but only leader can blaze one. That's often not easy. If you are a leader, a lot of people depend on you. Two options come with leadership: the temptation of serving oneself and the opportunity to serve the people you lead.

Leadership *'is about service, about shepherds who care for the shee'*. The word 'shepherd' communicates the love, nurture and spiritual care a godly leader provides. It involves both the rod (correction) and staff (direction). As mentioned earlier, Psalm 23 describes the shepherd's functions such as – provides necessities, confidently leads, guides and directs, loves unconditionally, protects from harm, corrects and comforts and provides shelter.

Nehemiah chose to be a servant-leader and it earned him enormous respect.

The characteristics of servant leader can be summarized:

'Mercy, peace and love be yours in abundance'

"All those who have authority, should use their power to lead; by taking orders from the Lord and serving those in need (D. De Hann.)"Leaders who serve will serve as good leaders.

Rehoboam crowned as king of Israel after the death of Solomon. The people were burdened by the harsh rule of Solomon and they pleaded with Rehoboam to be kind. Rehoboam consulted senior leaders of Solomon for their advice. The elders advised Rehoboam...

If you will be a servant to these people and serve them and give them a favourable service, they will be always being your servants' (Kings 11 and 12).

*Leadership is use of power to serve the people.*The truth is that the best leaders desire to serve others, not themselves. True servant leaderPut others ahead of their own agenda

• Possess the confidence to serve

• Initiate service to others

- Are not position-conscious

- Serve out of love

In short, a good Christian leader may serve as a visionary, influencer, passion infuser, team builder, victorious sufferer, fighter, helper and giver, determined man and woman of integrity, stabilizer, compromiser, encourager and servant-leader.

Let me conclude in the words of Walter C Wright:

I pray with Paul and Jude, asking God to fill you with the knowledge of his will through all spiritual wisdom and understanding... that you may live a life worthy of the Lord and may please him in every way; bearing fruit in every good work, growing in the knowledge of God, being strengthened with all power according to his glorious might so that you may have great endurance and patience, and joyfully giving thanks to the Father, who has qualified you to share in the inheritance of the saints in the kingdom of light. For he has rescued us from the dominion of darkness and brought us into the kingdom of the Son he loves, in whom we have redemption, the forgiveness of sins. (Col 1:9-14)

To him who is able to keep you from falling and to present you before his glorious presence without fault and with great joy – to the only God our Saviour be glory, majesty, power and authority, through Jesus Christ our Lord, before all ages, now and forevermore! Amen. (Jude 24-25) Alexander Strauch observes that our Lord repeated instruction on love, humility and servant hood, teaches us three important lessons:

1. God hates pride.

2. Christ's persistent teaching on love and humble servant-hood, demonstrate how difficult it is for people to understand and implement this principle.

3. Our Lord's repeated teaching shows that humility, servant-hood, and love are essential qualities of the Christian church.

Chapter 17

Spiritual Leadership[1]

God's children are reborn spiritually. (John 1:12-13)

There are many definitions of spiritual leadership; some think he is a "guru" and others as counsellor who can guide others through the problems and trails of life. *The Bible describes a spiritual leader as one who possesses the spiritual gifts of leadership, the ability to lead others as a direct result of the gifts received from and performed by the power of the Holy Spirit.* Spiritual leaders are also concerned with the souls of those they lead. The biblical spiritual leaders understand that their leadership is one of servant hood. Spiritual leaders lead by example, as Jesus did, who said He came to serve others, not to be served by them.[2]

> Not so with you, Instead, whoever wants to become great among you must be your servant, and whoever wants to be first must be your slave – just as the Son of Man did not come to be served, but to serve, and to give his life as a ransom for many. (Matthew 20:26-28)

A spiritual leader recognizes that he/she is first and foremost a servant. Jesus modelled the true servant style of leadership, when

He, the Lord incarnate, bent down and washed the feet of His disciples, teaching them that the true measure of a leader is one who first serves others.

> When he had finished washing their feet, he put on his clothes and returned to his place. "Do you understand what I have done for you?" he asked them. You call me 'Teacher' and 'Lord' and rightly so, for that is what I am. Now that I, your Lord and Teacher have washed your feet, you also should wash one another's feet. I have set you an example that you should do as I have done for you. I tell you the truth, no servant is greater than his master, or is messenger greater than the one who sent him. Now that you know these things, you will be blessed if you do them. (John 13:12-17) Obey your spiritual leaders and do what they say. Their works is to watch over your soul, and they know they are accountable to God. Give them reason to do this joyfully and not with sorrow. That would certainly not be for your benefit. (Hebrews 13:17)

The role of spiritual leader in the church is to...

> "equip the saints for the work of ministry, for building up the body of Christ" (Ephesians 4:12), and he concerns himself with doing just that. Spiritual leaders know that their main task is to sanctify the people of God and their prayer is the same as Jesus prayer to the Father.

> Sanctify them by the truth, your word is truth" (John 17:17).

> Like Jesus, the spiritual leader knows that the Word of God is the food of the soul and that it alone sanctifies. Rather than acquiescing to the "felt needs" of the people he leads, he shepherds others to maturity in the faith by speaking the truth in love so that those he leads "will in all things grow up into him who is the Head that is Christ. (Ephesians 4:15).

The spiritual leader must be spiritual. Spiritual leader connects their life with God first. Spiritual leaders in the church needs to care for the souls of those they lead, it does not mean that they should care for their physical needs. Spiritual leader's primary responsibility is leading them to spiritual maturity so that they will be fully equipped.

Spiritual leadership is one of the toughest forms of leadership. To lead someone to grow spiritually is an entirely different matter altogether.

James and John wanted the glory, but not the cup of shame, the crown, but not the cross, the role of master, but not servant. Jesus used this occasion to teach two principles of leadership that the church must never forget, the sovereignty of spiritual leadership and the suffering of spiritual leadership.[3]

Spiritual leaders are those who:

a. Have confidence in God rather than self-confidence,

b. Follow God's example closely rather than depend solely on one's own creativity.

c. Would lead by example rather than exercising control over others

d. Uses connection with God or prayer to get things done rather than use connection with others to get things done.

Sometimes leader's confidence become arrogance and loses humility. Leader has to balance their identity with their self-esteem. Look at how David perceived his identity and maintained both confidence and humility:[4]

a. David sees his own weakness and humanity

b. David sees his God-given position and privileges

c. David sees a balance by giving all the glory to God

A spiritual leader needs to get God's wisdom and understanding. It is essential that godly leader understand that[5]

- *God's vision is bigger than theirs*
- *They always include others in their work*
- *They want to see result and fruits*

- *They want to keep improving*
- *They want to see God's rule come to their organization and community*
- *They want to serve and add value to people*
- *They evaluate quickly and see possible answers*

> **It is better to lead from behind and to put others in front, especially when you celebrate victory when nice things occur. You make front line when there is danger. Then people will appreciate your leadership. - Nelson Mandela**

A spiritual leader should have the following traits of David as per John Maxwell.

- *Possess integrity*
- *Does not participate in gossip*
- *Does not harm others*
- *Speaks out against wrong*
- *Honours others who walk in truth*
- *Keep their word even at personal cost*
- *Is not greedy to gain at the expense of others*
- *Is strong and stable*

A Christian leader has to be a good shepherd and spiritually alert. A shepherd leader must be watchful, prayerful and courageous.

Roy Lessin describes how a godly leader....

- Finds strength by realizing his weakness
- Finds authority by being under authority
- Finds direction by laying down his/her plans
- *Finds vision by seeing the needs of others*
- Finds credibility by being an example
- Finds locality by expressing compassion

- Finds honour by being faithful
- Finds greatness by being a servant

> **God offers true spiritual fulfilment. (Isaiah 55:1-13)**
>
> **Only God can satisfy our spiritual thirst. (John 4:13-14)**

Spiritual discipline means living the way God wants us to. Jesus' moral standard seems high. But it is not to be reached by just our own ability. When we are Christ's, we are made into new creatures. The Holy Spirit lives through us as we become more like Jesus.

There are two reasons not to feel frustrated by the expectations we see here: First, eternal life is not earned but is God's gift. Second godly principles enable an individual to live stable, joyful lives.

What are the marks of true spirituality? Micah offers a summary by giving three virtues that are to characterize every one of God's people: to do justice, to love mercy, and to walk humbly with God (Mic. 6:8). This three sided approach to life is balanced, unlike many of the fads and fetishes of modern spirituality.

1. To act with justice keeps one in the real world rather than getting bogged down in theoretical abstractions that actually ignore oppression and injustice.

2. To love mercy keeps one in touch with the grace of a faithful God rather than succumbing to the tyranny of results-oriented spirituality, which tends to produce legalism, weariness and burnout.

3. To walk humbly with God keeps one dependent on God's resources rather than trusting in merely human solutions, which creates unrealistic pressure on individuals and institutions.

These three virtues are qualities that every believer needs not only to understand, but to practice.

Chapter 18

Christian Discipleship[1]

"All authority in heaven and on earth has been given to me.
Therefore go and make disciples of all nations,
Disciple is someone who believes and helps to spread the doctrine.
A disciple who is called to leadership needs to have right attitude.
A disciple should have servant attitude, like Jesus Christ.
"Your attitude should be the same as that of Jesus Christ"
(Philippians 7:5).

*T**he constant attendants of Christ can be called as Christian disciple,
as they profess to learn and receive Christ's doctrines and share with
others.* Christian discipleship is the process by which disciples
grow in the Lord Jesus Christ and are equipped by the Holy Spirit,
who resides in our hearts, to overcome the pressures and trials
of this present life and become more and more Christ like. This
process requires believers to respond to the Holy Spirit's prompting
to examine their thoughts, words and actions and compare them
with the Word of God. This requires that we be in the Word daily
– studying it, praying over it, and obeying it. In addition a Christian
disciple should give testimony of hope and disciple others to walk in

1. Putting Jesus first in all things (Mark 8:34-38)

2. Following Jesus' teachings (John 8:31-32)

3. Fruitfulness (John 15: 5-8)

4. Love for other disciples (John 13:34-35)

5. Evangelism – Making disciples of others (Matthew 28:18-20)

Christian discipleship is a concept that was born when Jesus Christ selected His first followers. A disciple, by definition, is a convinced adherent of a school or individual. In the case of Jesus, His disciples were those who followed Him while He was on earth, as well as those who continue to follow Him and His teachings today.

Christian discipleship is summed up in the Great Commission. After the resurrection and before He ascended into heaven, Jesus appeared one last time to His disciples. This is the moment that He delivered the famous calling for disciples known as The Great Commission:

All authority in heaven and on earth has been given to me. Therefore, go and make disciples of all nations, baptizing them in the name of the Father and of the Son and of the Holy Spirit, and teaching them to obey everything I have commanded you. And surely I am with you always, to the very end of the age (Matthew 28:18b-20).

Christian discipleship is more than being a believer. If you have chosen to follow Christ, then you are a Christian disciple! Thanks to the faithfulness of those apostles, who clearly understood their role as messengers of Christ, let us follow them, because this is the need of hour.

Chapter 19

Leadership and Prayer[1]

Again he prays and the heavens gave rain,
and the earth produced its crops (James 5:16-18)

rayer means a solemn request for help or expression of thanks addressed to God. For every Christian including Christian leader's prayer is the best way to communicate with God. It is said that prayer is the vehicle of dialogue with the creator. The best way to speak with God is prayer. Think for a moment that you have not spoken to your loved ones or a friend for some time. Your friendship and fellowship may not last long. Daily prayer is needed for closer and stronger fellowship with God. God likes us to be in constant conversation and share all our experiences, happiness, sorrows and problems. God wants to know all our activities at home and work place. The importance of prayer is mentioned over 250 times in the scripture. In the life of every Christian, daily prayer is crucial because:

- Prayer gives us an opportunity to share all aspects of our lives with God.

- Prayer gives us the chance to express our gratitude for the things He provides.

- Prayer provides the platform for confessing our sin and asking for help.

- Prayer is an act of worship and obedience.

- Prayer is a way to acknowledge who is really in control of our lives.

The scripture shows the power of prayer in the lives of great friends of God:

The power of a righteous person is powerful and effective. Elijah was a man just like us. He prayed earnestly that it would not rain, and it did not rain on the land for three and a half years.

Again he prays and the heavens gave rain, and the earth produced its crops (James 5:16-18).

God listens to prayer and answers.

Abraham prayed and God healed (Genesis 20:17). Moses prayed when people sinned and God heard him, strengthening his leadership (Numbers 21:7). Elisha prayed and the Lord opened the eyes of his young servant to see the power of God (2 Kings 6:17). King Hezekiah prayed and he was given a new lease of life that lasted for 15 years (2 King 20:1-21). Jonah prayed and he got out of trouble (Jonah 2:1). Daniel prayed and God helped him to remain faithful in a foreign land (Daniel 6:10). The disciples of Jesus prayed to get a new leader to replace Judas Iscariot (Acts 1:24-26). Peter prayed for "Tabitha who was dead and she sat up alive (Acts 9:40). A midnight prayer made the prison bars crumble for Paul and Silas (Acts 16:25). Paul prayed and healed a secular person (Acts 28:8). The best example, though, is from our Lord Jesus. He made it a habit to pray and often withdrew himself to solitary place (Luke 5:16). He prayed for his disciples as a group and for individual needs (Luke 22:32). And he prayed for strength when he had to go through Gethsemane (Luke 22:14-44).[2]

For Christian leaders, prayer can be challenging because Christian leadership demands to humble oneself on daily basis. God hears our prayer and acts His will through us. For every leader, prayer empowers and activates God's power to perform and fulfil our responsibilities efficiently and effectively. Unfortunately, some leaders are not serious about prayer or realise how little prayer actually goes in their lives. Let every leader 'ask', is prayer the first response for all thoughts, plans and actions in his/her leadership? Why don't you spend more time with God? What aspect of your time and commitment hold you back from prayer?

Chapter 20

Biblical Leadership[1]

Love God's call as passion.
Maturity that is needed to church and not to be to ourselves.

The church is born and continues to live by the people God chooses and the response we give. "I will be your God and you will be my people", is the relationship God calls us to – first to Himself and then to others. The church exists for us to be in Christ our Lord, to be His people, His hands, and His feet.

Leaders should not forget that the church they are leading is headed by Christ and He is supreme. This means He is head of the Church, He controls and guides.

The principles of God's call from the Bible to manage His flock!

Just as each of us has one body with many members and these members do not all have the same function, so in Christ we who are many form one? body and each member belong to all the others? We have different gifts, according to the grace given us. If a man's gift is prophesying, let him use it in proportion to his faith. If it is serving, let him serve; if it is teaching, let him teach; if it is encouraging, let him encourage; if it is contributing to the needs of others, let him give generously; if it is leadership, let him, govern diligently, it is showing mercy, let him do it cheerful. (Romans 12:4-8)

Managing a church needs true leadership. People confuse a strong willed personality as an effective leader, leadership is not being strong willed, rather having a strong sense of purpose that is cantered upon God. The church of our Lord needs leaders, not petty instigators. There are too many churches that substitute a petty person for a godly person and see no distinction, because the people who put them in power do not know the difference.

How effectively leaders manage their churches is crucial for its success. This largely depends on goal-setting strategies and budgeting ideas, designing constant meeting and action plans, and training leaders for/and congregation.

Biblical based leadership should have[2]

- A vision based on scripture, to hear and obey His word.
- Love God's call as passion.
- Energy to influence and being attractive for Christ
- Willingness to learn and grow from the experience of the Lord.
- Maturity needed for church
- Perseverance is to continue in his state of grace so he lives it out in our lives and walk with Christ
- Willingness to take a risk and go beyond himself. Have experience and knowledge and into what is best for the body of Christ
- No fear of failure is the ability to take a risk and keep the focus and attention on our call and obedience.
- Willingness to be follower, because he cannot lead where he has not been. Unless the leader is a good follower of the Lord, he cannot lead others effectively.

- Willingness to be a listener. He/she must know how, what and where to listen.

Biblical Leadership Characteristic[3]

Leadership that is based on Bible can be called as Biblical Leadership. Beginning from Adam and Eve in the Garden of Eden, we see different types of leaders. The leadership of Abraham, Moses, Joshua, Elijah, Elisha, David, Joseph, Kings and Judges, Prophets, and Apostles and other including Jesus, are few one can mention. A close study of these leaders will provide understanding of Biblical leadership traits and identify certain characteristics. Bible can give account of good and bad leaders and their consequences.

A leader, a group, a goal and a method to get the goals and results are important factors. The uniqueness of biblical leadership is that the entire process happens within the will, plan, priorities and purpose of Almighty God as revealed in the Bible, and is grounded, and operates under the lordship of Jesus Christ.

It is from this source that Christian leaders derive qualifications, objectives, principles and methodologies. In contrast, Nero, Stalin and Hitler may have been successful leaders, but they used principles foreign to the Christian faith.

Biblical leadership is about character development. Biblical leadership starts with a strong character. A person can have many skills and talents, yet without a fully developed character he will not be able to lead people in the direction they need to go. Many leaders in the Bible went through a wilderness experience to build necessary character before they were promoted to a place of leadership. Joseph spent 13 years in captivity, Moses 40 years in the wilderness, David spent about 10 years running from King Saul, John the Baptist came out of the wilderness and began preaching and Jesus was driven into the wilderness by the spirit to be tempted by the Devil before he began his ministry. These wilderness experiences show that God is very concerned about the character development of His leaders.

1. Self-Worth and Biblical Leaders

The first character a leader needs is a strong affirmation of who they are in Christ. If leaders are not convinced that they are a person of worth and have a healthy self-esteem, they may use their position of power to satisfy their deep-rooted insecurities. Jesus had a strong affirmation of who He was before He began His leadership and ministry.

2. Leader Must Be Able to Deal with Failure

In the Old and New Testament, many Biblical leaders seemed to fail miserably, but without their leadership, God's plan would not have been accomplished. For instance, Noah was a preacher for 120 years and only converted eight people; his self-worth could not have come from his success but must have come from his deep relationship with God. Moses faced many failures while leading Israelites to the Promised Land, which he could not see. His self-worth had to come from his intimate relationship with God to continue as a leader for forty years. Apostle Paul had many successes in his ministry but he also had many failures. Paul had an extremely good understanding of who he was in Christ which allowed him to overcome his failures and become possibly the greatest biblical leader of all time.

3. Biblical Leadership is About Trust

Trust is probably the greatest characteristic that a leader must build in biblical leadership. Without trust, people will not follow the leaders' vision. They will not put forth their full efforts and therefore the organization will never move in the direction a leader desires for it to move. Trust is built out of a strong character. First, a leader must trust himself/herself to lead effectively. Second, this trust must be developed through persistence. If a leader is not committed to see the vision through to its completion, they should never even mention it to those they are leading.

Nehemiah was a man with a vision to rebuild the wall around Jerusalem. He took his task and vision very seriously. His focus caused the wall to be built in record time, but it was not without threats or without setbacks. Nehemiah would not be satisfied until the wall was completed. *Biblical leadership not only builds trust through persistence but is also transparency.*

4. Biblical Leaders Keep Relationship with God First

A leader's character is extremely important to their effectiveness in Biblical leadership. Giving first place to God by giving maximum time, spiritual discipline, prayer, worship, Bible study and keeping Christ at centre are essential. These spiritual disciplines will give the leaders the affirmation of who is in Christ. This will resolve inner conflicts, it will help him grow in their emotional wisdom and build trust with those around him. Leaders never should become so busy that it affects their relationship with God. (Biblical inspirational .org)

Peter Nsowah has briefly summarized Christian methodology:

1. God gave original mandate to humanity; the Bible teaching about Christian leadership carries a narrower focus. Paul teaches that we have been given the "ministry of reconciliation" and "Therefore, we are ambassadors of Christ, as though God were entreating through us; we beg you on behalf of Christ, be reconciled to God."

2. Christian leadership highlights eternal matters over the temporary things of this world. We do what we can to make this life better. But in the final analysis, what good is it if we, for example, cure a person's cancer, yet let their soul slip into eternal hell?

3. Jesus asked the same question, "For what does it profit a man to gain the whole world, and forfeit his soul." (Mark 8:16)

4. The Bible teaching about Christian leadership portrays a unique method. As we walk through life, we actively spread God's values through our good example, persuasion and influence. Jesus called that as being salt of the earth, and the light of the world.

5. We also actively plan and program to persuade people to become followers of Christ. This is by persuasion, not by government decree or by the barrel of a gun.

6. Christian leadership also calls for a "servant" approach. Jesus modelled this approach when He taught the "Son of Man did not come to be served, but to serve and to give His life a ransom for many."

Christian leadership based on Bible teaching, is unique and valuable. Using Christian principles will greatly increase our success in life and work.

Chapter 21

Leadership Role as a Facilitator[1]

In short the facilitator's responsibility is to address the journey, rather than the destination. (Robert Bacal)

A facilitator is someone who helps a group of people understand their common objectives and assists them to plan to achieve them without taking a particular position in the discussion. Some facilitator tools will try to assist the group in achieving a consensus on any disagreements that pre-exist or emerge in the meeting so that it has a strong basis for future action. There are a variety of definitions for facilitator: An individual who enables groups and organizations to work more effectively; to collaborate and achieve synergy, is facilitator.

❝A facilitator is an individual whose job is to help to manage a process of information exchange, while an expert's role is to offer advice, particularly about the content of a discussion; the facilitator's role is to help with how the discussion is proceeding. In short the facilitator's responsibility is to address the journey, rather than the destination." (Robert Bacal).

Facilitator's job is to make it easier for the group to do its work, by providing non-directive leadership. The role is one of assistance and guidance not control. Good facilitation is hard work and it is difficult. Facilitators are supposed to be innovative and find their unique style and make different kinds of contribution to facilitation function.

A facilitator is one who helps to bring about an outcome by providing indirect or unnoticeable, invisible; assistance, guidance or supervision. Leadership is a process, not a position. Leadership is not focusing on one element but four elements – leader, follower and situation. The concoction (mixture) of these elements makes the leadership. Learning takes place when one interacts with fellow human beings and the situation. Taking the right direction in every situation is a challenging decision making process (Dr. Noah Balraj).

Facilitation by a leader is done based on one's personality. Facilitation enables:

- Building Credibility
- Communication
- Listening
- Assertiveness
- Conducting meetings
- Effective stress management
- Problem solving
- Improving creativity

A facilitative leader is one who is a leader in a group and his/her involvement is substantial in every issues. The expertise concerning the use is tremendous in both content and process expert. In decision making process he has final authority. On the other hand a facilitator is concerned only with the process. He/she acts as third party, neutral in all issues, only a process expert and does not act as a decision making authority.

We need to raise a new breed of leaders for the 21st century for church. Facilitators give place to others and eliminate competition within an organization. Facilitators need to look for God and value uniqueness of each person in Christ and do not demand authority. Facilitator should provide as quoted by CrokieHaan:

1. Deeper respect to all in an organization

2. Accountability towards each other and see that these will increase

3. Encourage collaboration in place of cooperation. Cooperation says, "Come, help me", while collaboration, "I want to be part of what God is doing"

4. Provide increased tolerance

In facilitation approach, not only is the decision that is made important, but also the way the decision is made. Facilitation is very crucial, especially when an organization is moving from authoritarian model to participative model. Here, leaders prefer to facilitate rather than give decisions. Facilitator leader has to play a consultative role rather than simply pass on information. This will encourage others to be more cooperative.

Competence and character of a facilitator is very important, as it is outlined by Institute of Culture Affairs, Canada.

1. Competence of a facilitator

- Distinguishes process from content
- Manages the client relationship and prepares thoroughly
- Uses space and time intentionally
- Is skilled in evoking participation and creativity
- Practiced in honouring the group an affirming its wisdom
- Capable of maintaining objectivity
- Skilled in reading the underlying dynamics of the group

- Releases blocks to the process
- Adapt to the changing situations
- Assumes responsibility for the group journey
- Demonstrates professionalism, self-confidence and authenticity
- Maintain personal integrity

The competence level of a facilitator can be judged depending on his analytical abilities, group dynamics, communication skills, inter-personal relations, self-management and technical abilities.

Character of facilitators

1. Asking rather than telling
2. Paying personal compliments
3. Willing to spend time in building relationships rather than always being task oriented
4. Initiating conversation rather than always having to offer someone else to
5. Asking for other's opinions rather than always having to offer his/her own
6. Negotiating rather than dictating decision-making
7. Listening without interrupting
8. Emoting (strong feeling e.g. anger) but able to be restrained when the situation requires it
9. Drawing energy from outside themselves rather than from within
10. Basing decisions upon intuitions rather than having to have facts

11. Has sufficient self-confidence that they can look someone in the eye when talking to them

12. More persuasive than sequential (a logical sequence)

13. More enthusiastic than systematic

14. More outgoing than serious

15. More like a counsellor than a sergeant

16. More like a coach than a scientist

17. Naturally curious about people, things and life in general

18. Keep the big picture in mind while working on the nitty-gritty

Phil Buttler suggests function of facilitator

1. Effective facilitators build trust, openness and mutual concern.

2. Lasting partnerships need a facilitator, someone who, by consensus, has been given the role of bringing the partnership to life and keeping the fires burning.

3. Successful facilitators develop a specific goal or task. This means lasting partnerships focus primarily on what (objectives) rather than how (structure).

4. Facilitators understand that partnerships are a process not an event

5. Facilitators take time and effort to develop an effective partnership. Effective partnerships do not come free.

6. Effective partnerships are even more challenging to maintain than to start. Facilitators make sure the vision stays alive, the focus is clear, communications are good and outcomes fulfilling

7. Facilitators assist their partner's ministries by developing clear identities and vision.

8. Effective facilitators acknowledge, even celebrate, the differences in their partner agencies histories, vision and services. But facilitators must ultimately concentrate on what they have in common, like vision, values and ministry objectives, rather than on their differences

9. Effective facilitators encourage a high sense of participation and ownership. The widest possible participation in objective setting, planning and the process of meetings and on-going communications is vital.

10. Effective facilitators expect problems and plan ahead for them.

The role of facilitator is crucial with following skills:

1. Setting goals
2. Providing constructive feedback
3. Team building for work teams
4. Building high-performance teams
5. Delegating
6. Coaching team members and employees

Spiritual Role of the Facilitator

I highlighted role of spiritual facilitator in servant leadership chapter. Here it is important to see the role of spiritual leadership. John Paul Jackson has explained role/characteristics of spiritual facilitator as follows:

1. A facilitator's authority comes not from titles of structural hierarchy but from God.

2. As facilitators are seen seeking the very heart of God, others will value their love for Jesus more than their denominational affiliation

3. Facilitators know the greatest changes in the church come through relationships. Relationships embrace a spiritual synergy when two or more agree. Then two can put ten thousands to fight.

4. Facilitators know that character doesn't come fast, nor does it come easy, but it last for a long time. Character is God's inoculation against the pride that comes when His power flows through mere humans.

5. Facilitators give their ministry to another knowing that they do not own it. Together the network is building what is God's. They have nothing to protect, and no reputations to uphold. Everything is now God's to kill or keep alive.

6. Facilitators know they have not earned their gifting and anointing and so are content with less public recognition.

7. Facilitators have the ability to minister without measuring success by size or numerical impact.

A leader is a facilitator of change. Bringing change is not an easy task; it requires high level of training, skills, patience and perseverance. Leadership is not a solo act; it involves the capacity to work with others. Leader's role includes that of facilitator to build the capacity of others and increase the chance of success.

God chose Moses not only as leader but also as a great facilitator to lead the Israelites. God is primary source for leadership role. Obey and love God to facilitate fellow human beings. Do unto others what you want others to do unto you.

Chapter 22

Leadership Accountability

As iron sharpens iron; so one man sharpens another (Proverbs 27:1)

*A*ccountability means responsibility for action. Hence, every leader is responsible for his action. *Accountability also requires a check and balance system to protect harm from ourselves and others.* While we are accountable, we are open to what we think and do so that we can receive encouragement and appreciation. Every Christian leader is responsible, answerable for his/her action in life. Christian accountability is accounting for what we are up to. It is the realization that we are liable, responsible and answerable for our actions in life to God. We need to hold to our beliefs and keep in line with what we believe, so it does not distract us from God's path for us or discourage others from their path.

When a leader is accountable, he/she allows being answerable to his/her family, friends, team members and organization. Accountability enables to share our lives with one another in deep, introspective way, enables to vent all frustration in life. Accountability is more of challenge than confrontation. Pride has no place when you are accountable. Accountability can encourage building and developing character, confidence, patience and dependence of team and God's grace. The call of God to take responsibility implies faithfulness and accountability to God and care for people. Paul understood that he was a leader and an influencer. He also understood his responsibility and to whom he was accountable.

If a leader is accountable, he/she can prevent physical stress and exhaustion. As per Dr. Richard J. Krejcir, effective accountability has the emphasis on building quality and deep relationships that will help with the following:

- *Adhering ourselves to God's word and call*

- *Learning to commune with God more deeply so we can respond to His precepts more rapidly and thoroughly*

- *Prayer that is not just about our personal needs but also with the needs of others*

- *Reigniting our passion for Christ*

- *Becoming teachable, and our thinking and behaviours examined*

- *Being willing to recognize sin both in our lives and in the lives of others too*

- *Being willing to learn about ourselves*

- *Being willing to have healing in our lives*

- *Being willing to see the needs of others*

- *Being willing to overcome and to be on guard concerning weaknesses and strengths*

- *Being able to trust, share and commune with another person in depth*

- *Being willing to overcome issues that are bad for us*

- *Knowing that we need others to keep us on track*

- *A willingness to be challenged, convicted, moulded and sharpened so we can change and grow*

- *Help to develop better and deeper fellowship and unity with others*

- *A platform to be transformed and renewed in Christ*

- *Becoming more sensitive and discerning*

- *Learning to develop the fruit of the spirit and exercise it*

- *Being willing to confess and hear others in love and confidentiality without judgment*

- *Being encouraged and encouraging others*

- *Developing godly, Christ - like character*

- *Learning to take risks, be vulnerable, and overcome rejection and betrayal*

- *Learning that God has called us to be involved in the lives of others and that we are not to be lone ranger Christians*

- *Learning that we are to be patient, because accountability is built over time*

- *Learning that deep connections do not just happen between services of the church, we have to work at them in community*

- *Learning that we are at our best when we are being real and authentic*

- *Learning about Christ's redemption and our ability to change*

- *Learning we can be used by God to be change agents in the lives of others*

- *Learning that relationships require effort and commitment*

- *Developing harmony with others so we can communicate and being transparent without being defensive*

- *Developing maturity and spiritual growth*

- *Learning to be humble and wise*

- *Allowing the work of the Holy Spirit within us and being used by Him in the lives of others as well*

- *The ability to bust the noise of our will and desires, as we need a godly perspective we can hear over that noise*

- *A reminder that God is in control, even in times of dire stress and confusion*

- *Trusting in God and keeping His standards because they are best for us, there is no better way than His Way*

- *Understanding that accountability takes place in the crucible of community with other growing Christians*

- *Knowing we need accountability for our support, faith development and growth*

- *Knowing that accountability takes our initiative, commitment and continuance in it.*

As iron sharpens iron; so one man sharpens another. (Proverbs 27:1)

Leaders have to adjust their Christian character for accountability, because character is the best measure of accountability Leaders who are not accountable, are the ones who will bring their organization/church bad reputation.

Collective responsibility provides genuine accountability. When there is genuine accountability, there is hope for breaking abuse of power.

Why do we Need Accountability?

According to Reji Samuel, accountability is a great quality that every leader needs to believe and practice.

- Accountability allows us to be answerable to one another

- Accountability enables us to share our lives with one another in a deep, introspective way

- Accountability helps instil the warning guideline that God has given us, but it also has the necessary support, counsel, encouragement and affirmation we all need

- Accountability enables us to be … in Christ, we who are many form one body; and each member belongs to all the others. This enables our connectedness to lay aside the isolated mentality

- All are tempted, accountability protect us from falling to the temptations

Calvin was especially a proponent of accountability and insisted all of his leaders be held in account, by honouring mutual righteousness among themselves, that they honour God. It was the system he established that became the model of the "check and balance" system of many modern governments.

The Methodist movement, founded by John Wesley, was started as an accountability and prayer group. Every effective minister, leader and growing Christian is in some form of an accountability group.

The success of our life and ministry depends upon relationships. The key to success is about learning how to manage our life and priorities. Leaders must know the skills necessary for leadership accountability. To be accountable is to be answerable to an authority outside of ourselves. It is to submit to a designated authority for the purpose of counsel, evaluation and responsibility with regard to our attitudes and relationships. Reji Samuel emphasizes the key skills for successful accountability:

- Trustworthiness
- Servant hood
- Perseverance

Practicing accountability is important but promoting it is very crucial for every leader.

Chapter 23

Abusive Leadership

There is but one just use of power,
and it is to serve people (George Bush)

*P*ower can be defined as *'control and influence exercised over others'*.
Authority is power that is legitimized and institutionalized
in a society or other social system. Power is the ability of
an individual or group to carry out its policies, and to control or
influence the behaviours of others, whether they wish to co-operate
or not (TitreAnde). It is a prerogative of a leader to have power
and authority. Leaders can decide how much and how they can use
their power. Leaders have choice, they can hold onto their power
and use it purely for selfish ends or they can give their power away
to others. Actually, leaders become more powerful when they share
their power. Leaders do not lose anything but everyone will benefit
when the power is shared. A leader's power is not reduced when
he/she empowers others. When power is shared, it actually expands
and multiplies. When team members have more responsibility and
can genuinely influence, their commitment to the organization will
increase, which will be successful. Authority requires responsibility. A
leader who gives an order is expected to be caring and responsible.

Too much power can lead to misuse leadership position. Leaders who are not using their power positively and abusing will act in a way which will be coercive and in extreme, could be bullying. Abusive power means badly or wrongly or even cruelly and violently, it can happen in the churches. Lord Acton says *"power tends to corrupt and absolute power corrupts absolutely."*

Pittacus wrote the measure of a man is what he does with power. The leader with abusive power will exhibit, "I need this, I deserve this, I demand this and I get this" By looking at David's life, we notice five common abuses of power. Calvin Miller describes them this way: (John Maxwell)

- Drifting away from those disciplines we still demand of our people
- Believing that others owe us whatever use we can make of them
- Attempting to fix things up rather than make things right
- Refusing to accept that we could be blindly out of God's will
- Believing that people in our way are expandable

Malcolm Webber study reveals following characteristics of abusive leader:

- They love to be first and seek the pre-eminence
- They refuse to submit to Godly authority.
- They gossip and slander others, especially those who are perceived as rival authorities.
- They are threatened by them
- The fear outside input and teachings
- They control the actions of those in their group

- They expel those who will not submit to their control (leadershipletters.com/abusive leaders)

Leadership will have two elements in an organization – position power and personal power. Organization gives position power which comes with jobs role and responsibility. The personal power is about the degree of influence the individual will have over his/her team. In practice, both are interlinked.

Jesus differentiated between world leadership and kingdom leadership. In Matthew 20:25-28, Jesus said that kingdom leadership is of a fundamentally different nature than the leadership of the world. Unfortunately, most Christian leaders as imperfect people, at some point exhibit character of abusive leadership. Abusive leaders are insecure and will have the character of self-absorption, self-protection and self-interest. Servant leaders are secure in Christ and their focus is not themselves but others. Servant leaders genuinely desire to empower and develop their followers. Their ultimate aim is to make them leaders. God calls spiritual or servant leader like Moses although Aaron was high priest and Miriam was prophetess.

A servant leader gives authority away to others, encourage participation in decision making, relies on other's knowledge and initiation for completion of tasks and depends on love and respect for influence. Abusive leader, on other hand, is one who tends to centralize authority and derive power from position, control of rewards and coercion. Use power to help people. For we are given power not to advance our own purposes, nor to make a great show in the world, nor a name. There is but one just use of power, and it is to serve people (George Bush).

In most cases church leadership has moved from biblical leadership to abuse power when:

- People are emotionally demeaned or low in dignity
- People are spiritually denigrated or criticized unfairly
- People are socially denied
- People are mentally dismissed
- People are physically dominated

Steps to Avoid the Abuse of Leadership Power

The abuse and misuse of power comes in the form of spiritual abuse, fraud, lying, greed, cheating, stealing, and decision based on fear, intimidation and exploitation of weak including sexual exploitation. According to Chris M. Coursry, this abusive power is the result of immaturity of a leader. Maturity helps to know our strengths and limitation and use power where and when necessary.

Chris M. Coursry identifies seven steps to avoid abuse of power:

- Assess maturity in your ministry and church leadership
- Address trauma or deeply distressing experience, in church leadership and those in authority
- Purposefully work on recovery while keeping the attention on the problems and potential for disaster.
- Address fear bonds in church structure and curb behaviours that enables leaders to go unchecked
- Use difficulties and trials as a litmus or acid test to see how maturity holds up in leadership
- Create an environment that promotes life – where leaders and congregants have accountability with team members who understand maturity.
- Be complete and address the Biblical concept of maturity today.

It is should be noted that most Christian leaders are imperfect and exhibit aspects of abusive leadership at some point of their leadership. Therefore, servant leader should follow the following steps as suggested by Malcolm Webber, so that they can be safe from abusive leadership:

- Prayer
- Study the example of Jesus Christ
- Humility
- Commitment to God
- Awareness regarding personal and organizational issues
- A good leader will be responsible for his follower's development
- Honestly and accurately assess or self-evaluation his own action and contributions
- Servant leader will exhibit genuine accountability

To aspire to leadership is an honourable ambition. (1 Timothy 3:1)

Chapter 24

Leadership Role in Youth Ministry

Youth is the reason of hope, enterprise and energy, to a nation as well as individual (W.R. Williams). At almost every step in life we meet with young men and women, and expect great and wonderful things. By nature, youth is bound to be 'miss-spent'; therefore, there is need for youth leaders to encourage, and build. A miss-spent youth may result in a tragic old age.

What is youth ministry?

Youth ministry is about reaching youth for Christ in such a way that they experience life change and become life changers. Youth ministries provide relationships, speak truth; includes scriptural truth, honest counsel and offer youth the purpose of life. Once we do this, youth will rise to take on the challenges of life and will be amazed to see what God does in their lives.

Why youth ministry is important?

Youth is the most impressionable age, which influences the rest of one's life, good or bad. Youth leaders and pastors have, therefore, special role in life of every youth in the church and community. Parents play important role, good or bad in the life of a youth. Youth leaders have to provide more than parents, by equipping their spiritual and social life. Building youth's life is a team work, of parents, youth leaders, pastors and elders in the church. It is not a difficult job as some believe, if we follow what God taught us about "loving God and loving people." One of the best things a youth leader can do is set an example, living life by 'loving God and loving people.

The future church depends on present youth. If church needs to be vibrant and grow, youth can do more and better with their gifts, talents, energy and commitment. Therefore, it is necessary for the churches to invest in youth ministry and retain youth membership. A recent survey by youth ministry indicated that 90% of any church's young people will drop away from church between the ages of 16 and 20, many will never return. Youth ministry therefore, should nurture youth spiritually, emotionally and socially, for the future of church. Today's investment on youth will decide the growth of tomorrow's church.

Youth today have to face the real world every day; we need to make sure that they are ready for the challenges. Youth leaders are required to provide those strengths to stand on their own faith and face the challenges of life. Many youth have been hurt, abused, and face problems of addiction and health. Youth leaders need to be honest, make sure the youth know that 'world is not a bed of roses' but full of trials. Building confidence to face reality of life and let youth know that they are not alone and have someone to listen and help is an important responsibility of youth leader.

Youth Leadership Qualities

Like Christian leaders, youth leaders need to have essential qualities such as – courage, visionary, change agent, decisive, perseverance, risk taking, creativity, confidence, self-discipline, honesty, and sense of humour.

Youth leader will have variety of tools like games and sports, sermons, seminars and camps to bring youth to Christ. These tools will have incredible impact and value in the life of youth. Youth also need training on time management. Youth leaders make sure that your youths know that you and your church care and love them.

Many great personalities of Bible inspire and teach lessons for Christian leaders. The lives of great men and women remind us that we too can make our lives fruitful and effective, including leaders. Let us see young leaders of Bible to emulate positively.

Jesus was aware that his mission would change the world, when he was just 12 years. From His life we learn sense of purpose and where you want to go. What you want do? How you can fulfil the vision of life to reality? Look for opportunities always.

David faced problem when he had to counter Goliath. David was a young man and inexperienced fighter while Goliath had a history as a great and violent fighter. David was not afraid, he was confident. He looked at the problem clearly and knew that he could not fight Goliath physically. Recognizing his limitations, he prayed and asked for God's help and finally he depended on the skills he had, to win.

What can we learn from David? The lessons a leader can learn from David are to have a cool mind, confidence, and courage, intelligent brain, not to give up and use skills efficiently and effectively according to the situation.

Joseph was a youthful dreamer and his dream came true. As a young man his mistake was being arrogant with his brothers, for which he paid dearly. What can we learn from Joseph's life?

- *Joseph was a slave but faithful so he won the confidence of his master.*

- *Joseph had physical beauty yet resisted temptation*

- *While he was falsely accused and faced unjust punishment, he showed patience.*

- *When he prospered, he was not proud and showed character of humility.*

- *Joseph was a man of wisdom, brotherly love and devotion to God.*

- *Joseph knew how to love and return good for evil.*

Ishmael was the eldest son of Abraham by his wife's slave Hagar. He grew up expecting to be the next leader of his father's tribe. Unexpectedly, Abraham's official wife Sarah gave birth to a son, when Ishmael was fourteen years old. The relation between Hagar and Sarah started to become uneasy. One day Sarah enraged and demanded that Ishmael and his mother Hagar be out of the tribe. Since she was the official wife, she wanted her son Jacob to be the heir of Abraham. Abraham loved Ishmael but listened to Sarah's demand and sent Ishmael and Hagar out in the desert.

Ishmael and Hagar were abandoned with no hope in a desperate situation when they headed towards Egypt. Hagar knew that was no chance that they would make it on their own. They were exhausted with no water. Ishmael succumbed to die and Hagar left him to die, because she did not want to see her son dying before her eyes. Ishmael did not give up easily. He prayed as his mother; and an angel of the Lord said; God heard the voice of the boy and I will make a great nation of him. Hagar opened her eyes and saw a well full of water.

The message here is clear that we should not give up, even when things look hopeless. Look for God in hope and faith, He will provide your needs and bless you.

Ruth and Orpah were Moabites married to Naomi's sons. Naomi was an Israelite. Naomi lost her husband and two sons. During famine, Naomi advised Ruth and Orpah to return to their families. Orpah followed Naomi's advice while Ruth did not abandon Naomi because she was old, alone and decided to stay with Naomi. Ruth said to Naomi,

> *"Where you go, I will go*
> *Where you Lodge, I will lodge;*
> *Your people shall be my people and your God my God*
> *Where you die, I will die*
> *There I will be buried*
> *May the Lord do this and so to me?*
> *And more as well*
> *If even death parts me from you.*
> Ruth 1:16-17

Ruth had a good sense to listen to Naomi and married a rich landowner. Ruth had a happy ending of courage and loyalty even in adverse situations. Ruth had a son Obed, who was the grandfather of King David.

From Ruth we learn to try to recognize good advice, and not to look desperate even when things look bleak. She kept her cool and trusted God; of course God rewarded her with His blessings.

Chapter 25

Leadership and Church

God does not want his people to live in isolation. The church is a spiritual community that can support us and help us grow in knowledge and faith.

The church exists for us to be in Christ, to be His people, His hands, and His feet. We are blessed to be blessings to others that are the purpose of life. God is our God; we are called to be His people. He has chosen us because He said "I will be your God and you will be my people." Every Christian needs to do their best at whatever job they are given in the church, and God will use them.

The church is growing at an extraordinary rate in many countries. The greatest challenge however, is lack of good and quality leaders.

Christians today criticize that the quality of leadership in churches are deteriorating and leaders do not understand modern world trends on the one hand, and on the other they see things in a worldly context in their leadership.

Today the church needs true and committed leaders who can have the following characteristics: (The Francis A. Schaffer Institute of Church Leadership Development)

The leadership challenges

- Have vision
- Have knowledge
- Love their call
- Be an Energizer
- Be a Learner
- Have Maturity
- Have Perseverance
- Have willingness to take risk
- No fear of failure
- Be a follower
- Be a listener

A healthy church needs a healthy leader, depending on new or old church. A leader needs to know how the healthy church looks like. Dr. Richard I. Kerjcir has given an overview of a healthy church by highlighting twelve characteristics:

1. The clear uncompromising teaching of God's Word
2. Impacting worship
3. Passion for the Lord
4. Heartfelt prayer
5. Making disciples
6. Penetrating love and care
7. Leadership development
8. Outreach and missions
9. Powered vision
10. Effective stewardship
11. Appropriate programming
12. Replication

Let Christian leaders know that the church does not exist in and for itself. It is the vehicle to lead and manage the people of God through discipleship, evangelism, missions, spiritual growth and programs for His glory and worship. Leaders must ask themselves, where they are and where their ministry is headed. All their efforts should be directed towards worship and just activities.

Christian leaders have multiple responsibilities. They have to:

- Share the word of God,
- Act as a shepherd and as a counsellor to build relations,
- Act as a manager to lead people where they need to go,
- Act as a teacher involving teaching on what a Christian is, how to grow in the faith and how to lead a Christian life.

When church leadership plans to grow their churches, it is necessary to identify for what God has called us to do and why? This includes leaders' focus on purpose, direction, method to make it work and things to avoid. Growth does not mean numerical growth but growth in faith and growth in Christ. Remember God likes such growth. The growth of church can be better if churches prepare pastor and church leadership to grow, implement hospitality, and lead the church in prayer.

Today's church leadership is facing new challenges around the world – unstable economic conditions, severe poverty and a dearth of competent and professional leadership in the church. Often people think that poor leadership in the church and lack of vision, skills and planning cause churches to limit themselves to spiritual aspects only. People need to develop a holistic ministry, where able and Godly leaders bring spiritual dimensions into the community, workplace, politics and economics. They want to see the church as productive as possible, with leaders having access to modern idea, technology and latest management principles.

As the churches grow, church leadership feel the pressure not only to produce growth in numbers but also to develop new programs. Unfortunately, in countries like India, church leaders are not well trained to manage large churches and develop a holistic approach to mission and ministry. There is a need for well-prepared leaders to effectively manage God established organizations to accomplish His purpose.

Without good leadership, the churches will continue to deteriorate and people will be directionless. Moses knew how important it was to have a leader to lead the people of Israel. He prayed to God to provide:

> Moses prayed to the Lord, "May the Lord, the Lord of the spirit of all mankind, appoint a man over this community to go out and come in before them, one who will lead them out and bring them in, so the Lord's people will not be like sheep without a shepherded" (Numbers 27:15-17)

Building leadership was Jesus' priority in his ministry. He chose his disciples and trained them not just as followers but to train others.

Today, churches and Christian organization need effective and godly leaders to nurture the church and its organizations. An effective leader has to be a continuous learner, continuous trainer and capacity builder of his/her colleagues or team members.

God does not want his people to live in isolation. Christians should not live in isolation (John 17:11). The church is a spiritual community that can support us and help us grow in knowledge and faith.

Chapter 26

Humanistic Leadership Role

What is Humanism?

It is a system of thought that centre on humans and their value, capacities and worth.

Humanism is a group of philosophies and ethical perspectives which emphasize the value, individually and collectively, and generally, prefers individual thought and evidence over established doctrine or faith. The term *humanism* can be ambiguously diverse, and there has been a persistent confusion between several related uses of the term because different intellectual movements have identified with it over time. In philosophy and social science, humanism refers to a perspective that affirms some notion of a "human nature". In modern times, many humanist movements have become strongly aligned with secularism, with the term *Humanism* often used as a byword for non- theistic beliefs about ideas such as meaning and purpose; however, early humanists were often religious.

What is leadership?

Webster on-line dictionary says *"a leader is one who directs on a course of action or in a direction"*.

In layman's terms, a leader is someone who has the courage to lead and the humility to help others.

A leader raises people's aspiration and encourages using energies to achieve their goals.

Leadership is important in every human activity in the human history.

As a leader you need to interact with your followers, peers, seniors and others, whose support you need in order to accomplish your goals. To gain their support you must be able to understand and motivate them. To understand and motivate people, you must know human nature. Human nature is the common qualities of all human beings. People behave according to certain principles of human nature.

What is Humanistic Leadership?
In the words of Jennifer Hancock:

- Humanistic leadership is an ethical philosophic approach that is at once: compassionate, reasonable and strategic

- Humanistic leaders are *compassionate*. They never forget that the people they are working with and for are real people with real strength, real weaknesses and most importantly, real emotions.

- Humanistic leaders are *ethical*. They don't just give lip service to their values. They actually live them and lead by example. No one wants to follow a hypocrite.

- Humanistic leaders are *reasonable*. They are willing to listen to dissenting views because they want to base their decisions on reality and not an assumption.

- Human leaders are *strategic*. They review all their options, consider the pros and cons of each solution and choose the one that will give them and their team the best chance of success.

Jennifer, in her definition highlights four *characteristics of humanistic leader* – *compassionate, ethical, reasonable and strategic.*

A leader was portrayed as a heroic figure with power, and usually a man – who gave commands.

Today thankfully, a leader is more than this; he/she is team builder with great leadership qualities. People expect a leader to have moral character and management skills. What is needed is a type of leadership that is motivated to respect fellow human beings, and seeing people, not as means but as ends in them. This constitutes humanistic leadership.

Humanistic leadership has to be hyper-local and focused on people. There is no universal and abstract method for dealing with people. Humanistic leadership should know that a good leader is not the one who believes in technique or skill alone but promotes social relationships. Humanistic leadership has to be sensitive to address people's problems and meet their expectations.

Humanistic Approach

In humanistic approach, leaders understand their role to provide freedom for an individual, to maximize their potential and become fit to understand humanistic leadership. Humanistic approach arises from a social-psychological foundation of democratic and individualistic values. McGregor wrote from humanistic perspective that saw the development of an individual is one of the key functions of a leader. McGregor, who invented Theory X and Theory Y, holds that people are not motivated and must be whipped and forced to work. Theory Y holds that people are intrinsically motivated and the leader needs to harness this pre-existing motivation to accept responsibility.

Burns (1978) originated the concept of *transformational leadership*. Transformational leader asks followers to move beyond their narrow self-interest, to develop themselves over a long term and to be aware of what is really important. When this happens, followers become leaders. The transformational leader is endowed with qualities that cause followers to accept the leader as a role model and as a person to be followed.

Around the 1990's, the term visionary leadership became popular. The *visionary leader* is he/she who translates those important purposes of an organization to the team in motivation ways.

Principles of Human Approach to Leadership

Leading people, based on human relationship principles, will prepare a leader to face many situations – comments, reactions, resistances, criticisms and misunderstandings. Human principles are like light houses that show you the right way in fulfilling responsibilities.

Jim Sellner highlights four principles of human approach to leadership:

1. Start with being person-focused – for the sake of both the employees/team members of an organization

2. Treat team members as collaborators, not as an object

3. Take a medium-to-long term perspective, not a bottom-line or short term perspective. Leaders should always think of how he/she can bring the best from team members and how can they help to develop unique abilities

4. Default (failure to do something required by law) to self-disclosure to create transparency. "Don't ask, why should I disclose this?" "Rather ask why not share it." Say "I have no secrets from you." Open up your desired outcomes, your constraints, your hindrances and insecurities – as

is appropriate to the situation. Let exchange be honest. Dishonest leader always face heat.

Characteristics of a Humanistic Leader

Jennifer, in her definition highlighted four characteristics of humanistic leader – compassionate, ethical, reasonable and strategic. I think humanistic leader is something more than this. Most importantly humanistic leader needs to be honest, hardworking, set an example to his/her team, display integrity and fairness, delegate responsibilities judiciously to his/her subordinates. Leaders should have ability to motivate and keep morale of his/her team always at peak. *Leadership is not wielding authority – it is empowering people* (Becky Brodin).

A successful humanistic leader, therefore, will have the following important roles or characteristics:

1. Humanistic leader as a visionary

A leader has to be practical and a realist yet must talk the language of a visionary and an idealist (Eric Hoffer). *Vision means the ability to think about the future with imagination or wisdom.* Leadership is about vision that empowers. Leadership is the capacity to translate vision into reality, offer hope for tomorrow and shape behaviour today. *"Where there is no vision, the people perish."*

The very essence of leadership (humanistic) is that you have to have vision; you can't blow an uncertain trumpet (Theodore M. Heshurgh).

- Vision without action is a day dream.
- Action without vision is a nightmare.
- Vision plus Action is Progress.

2. Humanistic leader as a determined person with integrity

Integrity is honesty and more. It refers to having strong internal guiding principles that one does not compromise. It means treating others as you would wish to be treated. *Integrity is the quality of being morally good.* In integrity one sees qualities which includes – honesty, dependability, uprightness, loyal and sincerity. Integrity springs from an individual's ethical and spiritual convictions.

The integrity of the upright will guide them,
But the crookedness of the treacherous will destroy them. (Proverbs 11:3)

King David writes in his prayer:

Let integrity and uprightness preserve me, for I wait for you (God)
Psalms 25:21

How many leaders have character of integrity?

For people who hate discipline (integrity) and only get more stubborn,
there will come a day when life tumbles in and they break,
but by then it will be too late to help them.
(Proverbs 29:1)

3. Humanistic Leadership has Love and Compassionate Heart

Love is a strong and positive emotion of regard and affection. Compassion means the humane quality of understanding for suffering of others and wanting to do something about it. R. M. Lala believes compassion is a deep feeling for and understanding of misery or suffering and the associated desire to promote its alleviation. Compassion is different from pity. Compassion connotes a greater dignity in the object of attention accompanied by an urgent desire to aid.

Humanistic leader, who has love and compassion, will have a character of generosity. Every leader has to be generous with their time and financial resources. A person can give without loving, but he/she can never love without giving. A humanistic leader must set an example through giving, so that everyone in their organization follows them. Generosity is an expression of love of God. Leaders, who are in love with God, will give their time and money to their people. Generosity includes love and compassion.

4. Humanistic Leadership as a Servant

Humanistic leaders try to forget themselves in the service of others. For when we think too much of ourselves and our own interests, we really become despondent. But when we work for others, our efforts return to bless us.

In the Christian realm, all leadership should be servant leadership. Servant leadership is best defined by Jesus Himself. Jesus said "whoever wants to become great among you must be your servant and whoever wants to be first must be your slave – just as the Son of Man did not came to be served but to serve and give his life, as a ransom for many."

In servant leadership one should be:

– Sense of call
– Put others ahead of their own agenda
– Posses confidence to serve
– Initiate service to others
– Not position conscious
– Serve out of love.

5. Humanistic Leader as Encourager

"Encouragement is the oxygen of the soul" (John Maxwell). Encourager is one who encourages, invites or stimulate to action, one who supplies incitement either by counselling or reward. While it is possible to lead without encouraging, good leaders have learned to use this important spiritual tool. The Bible commands us to encourage one another, and the leader should show the way in this area. Humanistic leaders are those who, through encouragement, can restore confidence and enthusiasm to a group of people who are discouraged and depressed. Nothing great has been achieved without enthusiasm. Good leaders are constantly reminding people of their value, of God's love, of the promises of Scripture, and that failure is not the end of the world. Since followers are bound to fail often, the role of encourager, while not owned exclusively by leaders, is crucial to leaders' ability to maintain morale. Encouragement coming from a leader often has more impact for good than that coming from others. The world belongs to the enthusiast who keeps cool. A real leader, through actions and words, has ability to encourage and motivate others to their highest level of achievement; gives them the opportunity and freedom to grow.

The task of leadership is not to put greatness into people, But to elicit it, for the greatness is there already (John Buchan)

6. Humanistic leader as democrat

A leadership style is a leader's style of providing direction, implementing plans and motivating people. Different situation calls, for different leadership styles. The style adopted should be the one that most effectively achieve organization goals, taking into consideration the interest of the member of organization.

There is vast difference in the various leadership styles. The basic types are – Autocratic, Democratic and Laissex-faire. If leader has to follow humanistic leadership he has to be democratic. In democratic style, the entire group shares in decision making. This style encourages team work, where team comes for a collective decision. In this type, everyone's opinions are taken into consideration. The disadvantages caused by autocratic style are ruled out in this style.

This style is also known as participative leadership style.

Moses, Joshua, Nehemiah and David can be best example of humanistic leadership, all of them had this quality therefore, and they were successful in leading their people.

Apart from these characteristics, humanistic leader should have qualities such as – influencer with value, willing to suffer, willingness to compromise, right and positive attitude and intelligent and wise.

Investing in Future Humanistic Leaders

Being a leader is an important job, although it is not easy. The world needs leaders who are not managers of people, money and organizations but leaders with human touch. Leadership is always crucial to any organization like church, society and country. *It seems to me that we have first class problems and second class leadership.*

Leadership is important in every human activity in the human history. Leaders need to have all the best qualities, more they needed to be leaders with a humanistic approach.

To be a successful leader in this dynamic and volatile society is not easy. Leaders are to be prepared. Therefore, well thought training and development is very essential, which demands investment in terms of money and time.

Great organizations do not just happen. You need a leader and a team with proper training. Some of the best leaders are those who have been taught how to be efficient, effective and have a human touch. Investing in training will bring the following benefits to a leader, team and organization:

1. It brings good work culture
2. It will help each member, even the leader of an organization to know his/her task, role and responsibility

3. It will bring harmonious relations in an organization, which is essential for humanistic approach

4. Leader and members will learn to know their leadership qualities. Sharpen their skills and even human behaviour

5. It will allow to keep up with time and latest development

6. Finally, it will teach how to become humanistic leaders

Consider Mother Teresa, being humanistic leader without power and status, received appreciation and respect from around the world. To be humanistic leader, you need to have *characteristics* like:

1. Character that enables us to do what is right even when it seems difficult

2. Perspective that enables us to understand what must happen to reach a goal

3. Courage that enables us to initiate and take risks to step out towards a worthy goal

4. Favour that enables us to attract and empower others to join us in the cause.

Therefore, it is crucial to invest in evolving leaders with human touch.

PART 3

Developing Leaders and
Leadership for an Organization

Chapter 27

Organizational Development

Leadership development is a life time journey-not a brief trip. John Maxwell

It is the responsibility of a leader to develop leaders and leadership for an organization. It is urgent for churches and Christian organizations today.

Anyone can follow a path, but only a leader can blaze. This is not often easy. If you are a leader, I hope you are all leaders in your own way. A lot of people need and depend on you: family and friends, communities, churches and your organizations. As others depend on you, on whom can you depend? The answer is God, the ultimate Leader!

Organization's or church's present and future depends upon the leader. Leadership ability is the lid on the success of organization. A leader influences his/her organization and the team; effectively achieve a defined mission together. Three key words stand out in this definition – influence, effectiveness and togetherness

A leader as an influencer must accomplish five tasks; each task requires five leadership skills:

1. Leader influence others by embodiment – as a model for imitation.

2. Leader influences others by education – as a mentor for instruction

3. Leader influences and inspires new leaders by empowerment - as a motivator for inspiration

4. Leader as influencer is equipping for the implementation – as a good manager.

5. Leader's final challenge is evaluation for the purpose of improvement – as a minister

The second key word for developing leader is *effectiveness or efficiency.* Christian leadership first promotes faithfulness then effectiveness. Efficiency is useless if you are not effective and to be effective requires faithfulness.

The following *four steps* can achieve the development of future leaders – *Faithful, Effective and Efficient.*

1. The principle of effectiveness: learning to do the right things

2. The principle of excellence: learning to do the right things in the right way

3. The principle of efficiency: learning to do the right things in the right way at the right time

4. The principle of exaltation: learning to do the right things in the right way at the right time for the right reason.

When a leader influences others, to effectively achieve a defined mission, then people will come together and form a team. There are *three powerful and unifying team building dynamics:*

1.   A unified motivated team has to accept the team leader

2.   Bringing people together is unified acceptance of the team's defined mission.

3.   It is also crucial for team members to accept one another

Leaders are marked by the ability to influence others, to effectively achieve a defined mission together, but of necessity they also have absolutely non-negotiable personal qualities required for long-term effective leadership. Your thoughts determine your character. The first person you lead is you. Christian leadership is a privilege, not a right.

Organizational Development and Leadership

One of the greatest gifts leader can give to those around them is hope. Never underestimate its power.

Organizational development is *defined* as "collaborating with organizational leaders and their groups to create systemic change on behalf of root-cause problem-solving toward improving productivity and employee satisfaction through strengthening the human processes through which they get their work done."

Leadership training has a direct *impact* on organizational development, because the more a leader is developed with leadership skills and overseeing an organization, the more the organization as a whole will change. If the leadership in an organization does not deal with feedback very well, the entire organization may develop fear of voicing their opinion. In leadership training, the proper education of how to deal with feedback and organization conflict can provide a more balanced perspective on feedback, changing the organization culture and feeling the employees to provide honest feedback.

Proper leadership training coupled with movement in organization development will in effect directly result in satisfied employees, more productivity and a positive working environment. Organizational development has a specific emphasis on human behaviour as a result of an organization's health. As organizational development aligns more and more with the employee's needs and desire, the more productive that organization will be.

Organizational development is implemented by leadership. Organizational development and leadership play a vital role with one other. A leader carries the authority to directly affect an organization's policies and procedures that influence the organization culture and effectiveness. Without effective leadership, organizational development will falter or lose strength, ending disgruntled employees, counter-productive procedures and ineffective business practices.

Organizational development is defined as "an effort, planned, organization-wide, and managed from the top, to increase organizational effectiveness and health through planned interventions in the organization's processes, using behavioural-science knowledge."[2]The purpose of leadership in organizational development is to influence human resources, create positive change in the working environment, and remains in global markets and to expedite organizational change. Human resources takes care of employees personal needs, directly affecting the company. Leadership also uses organizational development as a method of correcting negative aspects of corporate culture and fosters trust and loyally among workers. When leaders are participating in organizational development, positive change happens faster and more efficiently.

Organizational development is a process that has specific steps that are accomplished. In the beginning, the leadership identifies the needs in the organization that require change. The leadership collects the data and encourages feedback from professionals in the field and employees. Considering the feedback and the findings of leadership, an action plan is implemented that details the steps required making the organizational change. After implementing the action plan, the leadership assesses the effectiveness of the changes and then adjusts the action plan for the most effectiveness.

Leadership that plays an active role in organizational development results in a positive culture, employees who trust leadership and a productive working environment. The results of organizational development increase effectiveness, therefore, increasing success.

In order for organizational development to be effective, a team of various leaders need to be developed. This team should include external and internal leadership such as staff, board members, advisors and all levels of management – lower, middle and upper. It is important to include leadership that has experience in organizational development for an accurate and objective assessment.

Leadership Development matters

Professor David Perkins has dealt with challenges for developing leadership in an organization. He also dealt with what steps should organizations take to improve the effectiveness of their leadership development. The Learning Innovations Laboratory of Harvard University suggests that *successful leadership development depends on*:

1. Focusing on the development of leadership, not individual leaders

2. Distributing leadership responsibility throughout an organization

3. Embedding leadership development in the context of people's work

4. Assessing your organization's capacity for, and immunity to, leadership development

There is still lack of consensus about what constitutes leadership for an organization? However, it is agreed that developing leaders and leadership is a sure means of transforming organization for better. So, leadership development matters.

Leadership is more art than science. The principles of leadership are constant, but the application changes with very leader and every situation.

Issues Involved in Organizational Leadership

John Maxwell believes *"everything rises and falls on leadership."* Organizational leadership is the official authority that governs a group of people. The leadership structure can vary, depending on organization's philosophy. It can use an authoritative or democratic approach.

Leader holds the responsibility to train, develop and provide direction for a team. Organizational leadership is the person or people established to govern and have authority over, a particular business, government or organization. The leadership over an organization sets the tone of the organization culture, expectations and the vision. Various leadership issues can arise in organizational leadership that can hinder the organization's effectiveness and results. Identifying and addressing the organizational issues is the first step in resolving the issues and implementing positive change. The major issues involved in organizational leadership are (Nicole Papa):

1. Lack of involvement

Lack of involvement of the leadership can cause employees to feel as if upper management does not care about the daily affairs. One of the best ways to motivate people is for leadership to first do what it wants others to do. This mirroring method is effective because subordinates are looking to the leadership to demonstrate the principles and expectations of the organization.

2. Lack of communication

Communication is the exchange of ideas, thoughts and information through actions, words and symbols. Organizations use two types of communication: upward communication and downward communication. Upward communication is when subordinates send message to those above them. Downward communication is sending messages from management to subordinates. When communication lacks from leadership, subordinates are left without direction and purpose and lose motivation to perform their daily tasks well. Lack of communication can manifest in lack of spoken words or action from the leadership.

As a leader, your communication sets the tone for interaction among your people.

3. Inability to provide feedback

Organizational leadership that does not provide opportunities for subordinates to provide feedback is limiting their ability to implement change. Without feedback, subordinates may feel limited, restricted and disrespected. Feedback gives a voice to followers in an organization so they feel like they play a role in the decisions that are made and overall success of the organization. Feedback provides the followers with a sense of purpose and a personal investment in the organization. Implementing an "open door policy" can help encourage subordinate to share their concern, ideas and desires to leadership.

4. Ineffective leadership style

The use of wrong leadership style in an organization can hinder the success of the organization. For example, if the military used a democratic leadership style where subordinates are encouraged to question directive, wars would not be won and orders would take too long to follow. An authoritative leadership style is appropriate for military leadership where a command is given and followed without question. In an organization a democratic leadership style would empower free-thinking, conceptual thinking and problems solving.

One of the greatest gifts leader can give to those around them is hope. Never underestimate its power.

Leadership training for organizational development[3]

Leadership training is essential for successful and effective.

Organizational development. Leadership training provides a consistent training and development program that enables leaders to recognize their strengths and weaknesses in order to utilize a leader's strong points and build areas of weakness. An important aspect of leadership training is organizational

> *But select capable from all the people-men who fear God, trustworthy men who hate dishonest gain-and appoint them as officials over thousand, hundreds, fifties and tens.*
> *(Exodus 18:21)*

development where the leadership assesses its current organizational structure and provides suggestions on how to improve an organization flow.

The leadership training is the *process* of empowering, educating and providing tools for those given authority over a group of people.

Organizational development is *defined* as "collaborating with organizational leaders and their groups to create systemic change on behalf of root-cause problem-solving toward improving productivity and employee satisfaction through strengthening the human processes through which they get their work done."

Leadership training has a direct impact on organizational development, because the more a leader is developed with leadership skills and overseeing an organization, the more the organization as a whole will change. If the leadership in an organization does not deal with feedback very well, the entire organization may develop fear of every voicing their opinion. In leadership training, the proper education of how to deal with feedback and organization conflict can provide a more balanced perspective on feedback, changing the organization culture and feeling the employees to provide honest feedback.

Proper leadership training coupled with movement in organization development will in effect directly result in satisfied employees, more productivity and a positive working environment. Organizational development has a specific emphasis on human behaviours as a result of an organization's health. As organizational development aligns more and more with the employee's needs and desires, the more productive that organization will be.

> *"Failing organization are usually over-managed and under led."*

An effective way to implement change organizationally is to have assessment performance in your organization. An assessment takes on objective look at the organization, identifying strengths and weaknesses and provides an action plan, to fill in the gaps of the weaknesses. This helps to develop the leadership team and provide on objective look at how successful the organization is.

Chapter 28

Leadership -
Christian Perspective for a
Christian Organization[1]

God has promised His guidance.

I will lead them in paths they have known. I will make darkness light before them, and crooked places straight. These things I will do for them, and not forsake them (Isaiah 42:16).

The call to leadership is a consistent pattern in the Bible. When God decided to rise up a nation of His own, He didn't call upon the masses. He called out one leader – Abraham. When He wanted to deliver His people out of Egypt, He did not guide them as a group. He rose up a leader to do it – Moses. When it came time for the people to cross into the Promised Land, they followed one man, Joshua.

For Christian leaders, it is important that they *value the mission and vision* of their organization, because it energizes. He/she who has no mission or vision is the poorest of all. David's vision energized the Hebrew nation far beyond anything Saul had ever imagined. David's vision for the Israelite nation was a great blessing, the same

1. Vision united: For the first time in years, all the tribes and all the elders came together

2. Vision provides a centre for leadership: David began his reign from Hebron, but desired to unite a divided land and lead from Jerusalem

3. Vision dominates inner conversation: All of us indulge in inner conversation. David's vision focused on his men as they neared Jerusalem

4. Vision inspires greatness: David's dream for Jerusalem helped him and his people realize a great goal together

5. Vision attracts others to the leader: Once David had taken Jerusalem; others began to join the cause.

Denis Waidey says, *"The winner's edge is not in a gifted birth, in high IQ, or in talent. The winner's edge is the attitude not aptitude."* John Maxwell rightly described how various attitudes impact a team or organization. The positive attitude of a leader is necessary to bring positive change in his organization. It depends on how you look at things and not how they are. Your new attitude might improve your career opportunity and prospect.

Abilities +	Attitude	=	Result
Great Talent	*Rotten Attitude*		*Bad organization*
Great Talent	*Bad Attitude*		*Average organization*
Great Talent	*Average Attitude*		*Good Team organization*
Great Talent	*Good Attitude*		*Great organization.*

No organization can *change* unless leader changes and/or positive priorities.

Be transformed by the renewing of your mind (Romans 12:2).

Everyone agree that growing or change is good, but few actually dedicate to the process. Because growth requires change and change is hard for most people. But the truth of the matter is without change growth is impossible. Most people fight against change, especially when it affects them personally. As Leo Tolstoy said, "Everyone thinks of changing the world, but no one thinks of changing himself." Everybody has to deal with change in their lives. Remember people unwilling to change will never reach their potential.

There are two kinds of leaders: those who *attract followers* and those who *attract leaders*.[2] Leaders who attracts followers will never be able to do anything beyond what they can personally supervise. Look for leaders who attract other leaders. They will be able to multiply success. To keep attracting better and better leaders, you will have to keep developing your own leadership abilities. Be nice to people (in your organization) on your way up because you will meet them on your way down.

Everyone believes that *investing* in a team will benefit everyone and organization. One of the great things about investing in a team is that it almost guarantees a high return for the effort, because a team can do so much more than individuals. *"Venture a small fish to catch a big one."* Rex Murphy said: *"Where there is a will there is a way, where there is a team there is more than one way."*

In an organization you are able to get people to go with you, when you find out where they are, move towards them to make *contact and connect* with them. If you can do this successfully, you can reach new heights in your relationship and development in organization.

In an organization, it is the team leader's responsibility to orchestrate the *team's growth.* He/she must make sure that his/her people grow both personally and professionally. He/she must insure that their growth happens with them together – as team. Shared experiences and the give-and-take and communication are the greatest ways to promote team growth.

When a leader called by God has too much responsibility and cannot handle it, *God provides* help, if the leader asks for it. Not only does God provide helpers to share the responsibilities, He will also bless/anoint them with His power, as he did the seventy elders of Israel for Moses (Exodus 24).

Remember the road to biblical leadership comes through *service*. Leaders may find themselves in the spotlight, but they also take the heat, that often comes with the place of prominence. They speak up for the sake of the mission, but they are also willing to remain silent when it serves the organization. And at any movement they must be willing to make all kinds of sacrifices for the sake of people and organization.

Great leaders have to spend long years before they take up leadership role. They have to wait till God trains and allow them to take up leadership responsibilities. Joseph waited nearly twenty three years, from pit to the palace and fulfils his vision or dream. Self-promotion with his brothers failed. Joseph realized self-promotion can never replace God's promotion. A leader has to depend upon God to prepare and grant an opportunity to lead.

It is very unfortunate to see Christian organizations today are losing energy, becoming weak, inefficient, losing effectiveness, lacking commitment, lacking passion and sincerity. The most serious issue is lack of sincere, committed and efficient leaders. I am sure this presentation which I dealt from management and Christian perspective for Christian leaders will help. Your leadership ability always determines your effectiveness and the potential impact of your organization.

Endnotes

Chapter 1
[1] Mike Murdock, *The Leadership Secrets of Jesus,* Authentic Books, 2008, p.143.

Chapter 2
[1] As mentioned by John Maxwell, Leadership Promises For Every Day, p.49:

[2] John Maxwell, *Leadership, Promises For Every Day*, p.151

[3] John Maxwell, *Leadership, Promises For Every Day*, p.336.

Chapter 4
[1] Lela, In Search of Ethical Leadership, pp.59-60.

[2] John Maxwell, *Leadership, Promises For Every Day*, p.72.

[3] Andy Stanley, The Next Generation Leader, Authentic Headlines, 2003, p.58.

[4] Ken Blanchard, as mentioned by John Maxwell, Leadership, Promises for Every day, p.3.

[5] John Maxwell, *Leadership, Promises For Every Day*, p.382.

Chapter 5
[1] Hisn-Yi Cohen, *Leadership in Dealing With Conflict*, 2012, *www.leadershipexpert. com.co.uk*

[2] *Richard Branson*, Leadership and Conflict, 2011, *5cblog.wordpress.com*

[3] *Richard Branson*, Leadership and Conflict, 2011, *5cblong.wordpress.com*

[4] *Hsin-Yi Cohen*, Leadership in Dealing with Conflict, 2012, *www.leadershipexpert. com.co.uk*

Chapter 6

[1] John Maxwell, *Leadership, Promises For Every Day*, p. 111.

[2] John Maxwell, *Leadership, Promises For Every Day*, p. 188.

Chapter 7

[1] R. M. Lala, *In Search of Ethical Leadership*, p.93

[2] Doug Britton, *Understanding the Meaning of Humility in the Bible*, 2008, *www.DougBrittonBooks.com*

[3] Kenneth Boa, *Humility*, *www.kenboa.org commentary*

[4] R. M. Lala, *In Search of Ethical Leadership*, p.93.

Chapter 8

[1] Read Volume 1 on leadership by John Zechariah.

[2] R. M. Lala, *In Search of Ethical Leadership*, p.32.

[3] R. M. Lala, *In Search of Ethical Leadership*, p.30.

[4] R. M. Lala, *In Search of Ethical Leadership*, p.31.

Chapter 9

[1] *Refer also chapter 14, 15, 16 of this book.*

[2] John Maxwell, *Leadership, Promises For Every Day*, p..19.

[3] *As mentioned by Job Byler, The Art of Christian Leadership*, p.14.

[4] *As mentioned by Jon Byler, The Art of Christian Leadership*, pp.15-16.

Chapter 11

[1] Jon Byler, The Art of Christian Leadership, pp.45-47.

Chapter 12

[1] Refer John Zechariah's, paper on Christian Leadership Training, Asian Academy for Leadership and Peace (AALP), India, 2012.

Chapter 13

[1] Peter Nsowah, *Shepherd Leadership, Christian Discipleship, National Christian Youth Leadership Training-Spiritual and Secular Perspective, AALP, India*, 2014.

[2] John Maxwell, *Leadership, Promises For Every Day*, p.204.

Chapter 14

[1] Mohanraj Israel, Servant Leadership, Christian Discipleship, National Christian Youth Leadership Training-Spiritual and Secular Perspective, AALP, India, 2014.

[2] Malcolm Webber p.24.

Chapter 15

[1] Robert Donald, *Characteristics and Qualities of Leadership, National Christian Youth Leadership – Spiritual and Secular Perspective*, AALP, India, 2014.

[2] John Maxwell, p.238.

[3] Malcolm Webber, p.39.

Chapter 16

[1] Mohanraj Israel, Servant Leadership, Christian Discipleship, National Christian Youth Leadership Training-Spiritual and Secular Perspective, AALP, India, 2014.

Chapter 17

[1] *John Zechariah, Spirituality and Responsible Leadership for Christian Youth Ecumenical Centres of Asia, Association of Christian Institute of Social Concern, at KKFI, Manila, Philippines, 2008)*

[2] *John Zechariah, The Role of Christian Spirituality: Empowering Poor Communities, Association of Christian Institute of Social Concern*, at KKFI, Manila, Philippines, 2010.

[3] Oswald Sanders,

[4] John Maxwell, p.215

[5] John Maxwell, p.277.

Chapter 18

[1] Reji Samuel, *Christian Discipleship, National Christian Youth Leadership Training-Spiritual and Secular Perspective*, AALP, India, 2014.

[2] Got Questions Ministries

Chapter 19

[1] John Zechariah, Paper presented at Christian Leadership, *Spiritual Perspective*, AALP, 2014.

[2] Titre Ande, p.53.

Chapter 20

[1] Peter Nsowah, *Biblical Leadership, National Christian Youth Leadership – Spiritual and Secular Perspective*, AALP, India, 2014.

[2] The Francis A. Schaffer Institute of Church Leadership Development.

[3] Peter Noswah, *Biblical Leadership, National Christian Youth Leadership – Spiritual and Secular Perspective*, AALP, India, 2014.

Chapter 21

[1] Noah Balraj, *Leadership Role as a Facilitator, National Christian Youth Leadership – Spiritual and Secular Perspective*, AALP, India, 2014.

Chapter 28

[1] John Zechariah, *Christian Leadership Training, Spiritual Perspective*, Asian Academy for Leadership and Peace Seminar (AALP), India, 2013.

[2] John Zechariah, *Christian Leadership, Opening Address, National Christian Youth Leadership Training-Spiritual and Secular Perspective*, AALP, India, 2014.

Recommended Books/Resources For Your Further Reading

Adrian Russell, 2011- *Paul's Leadership Essentials, The briefing*, matthiasmedia.com

Alexander Strauch – *Biblical Eldership*

Ajit Fernando- *Leadership Lifestyles*

Andy Stanley – *The Next Generation Leader*

Autry J – *Love and Profit: Finding the balance in life and work*

Bernard Grant – *First Class Leaders, Fifty Principles for Becoming a Strong Leader*

Biju Michael, sdb – *Leadership Success the Real Way*

BrucGoettsche; 1988, *Principles of Effective Christian Leadership*, www,unionchurch.com

Chris M. Coursey – *Seven Steps to void the Abuse of Power (article)*

CorckieHaan – *Facilitator: A New Role for Church Leader?*

Dennis McCallum – *Areas of Leadership Responsibility*

Dennis McCallum – *What is a Christian Leader?*

D. Quinn Mills-*How to Lead, How to Live Leadership*

Elizabeth Fletcher, 2006, *Ruth in the Bible – Loyal to Naomi and faithful to God*, www. womeninthebible.net

Graham Yemm – *Leadership – Do you use or abuse power?*

Greenleaf R.K – Servant Leadership

Henry S. Givery – *12 Distinguish Qualities that Define True Leaders*

Henry S. Givery – *10 ways to become a Better Leader, Improve Your Leadership Skills*

Herbert Lockyer – *All the Men of the Bible*

Herbert Lockyer – *All the Women of Bible*

Isaksen S. – *Facilitative Leadership: Making a difference with creative problem solving.*

John Byler – *The Art of Christian Leadership, Developing Skills to Lead God's People*

John C. Maxwell – *Leadership – Promises for Every Day*

John C. Maxwell – *Be a People Person*

John C. Maxwell – *Leadership 101, Inspirational Quotes and insights for Leaders.*

John Macarthur – *The Book on Leadership*

John Macarthur – *Twelve Ordinary Man*

John Paul Jackson – *The Spiritual Roll of the Facilitator*

John Zechariah – *Ecumenical Leadership*

John Zechariah – *Leadership and Spirituality*

John Zechariah – *Papers on Leadership*

J. Maurus – *A Source-Book of Inspiration*

J. Oswald Sanders – *Spiritual Leadership*

KathyrynCapoccia, 2001, *Naomi: A Woman Who Learned to Believe in God's Providence*, *www.bibleb.com*

KathyrynCapoccia, 1978, *Woman Bible – Ruth*, New York Bible Society, Zondervan Bible Publication

KathyrynCapoccia- *A Woman of Courage a Faith, Women of the Bible – Esther*, *www.bible.com* and *www.gospelgems.com*

Kendra Cherry – *10 ways to become a Better Leader*

Lynne Chapman- *Lesson from the Bible – The book of Esther*, Christian Living Site, BellaOnline's Christian Living

Mark Conner-*Leadership Lesson from King David*, Leadership Summit May 1, 2008, City Life Sermon notes.

Mark Shed – *Leadership Quotes*

Malcolm Webber – *Abusive Leadership, Spirit Build Leadership6*, Strategic Press, USA, 2002

Malcolm Webber – *Building Leaders, Spirit Leadership 4*, Strategic Press, USA 2002

Mike Murdok – *The Leadership Secrets of Jesus*

Noah Balraj - *Leadership Role as Facilitator from Christian perspective* (Paper presented at AALP January 2014)

Pam Dewy- *Book of Esther Bible Study*

Peter Nsowah – *Shepherd Leadership* (Paper presented at AALP January 2014)

Per Winbladh, *Leadership Lessons from King Solomon*, the Swedish American Chamber of Commerce Currents, October 4, 2010

Phil Butler - *Partnership: Accelerating Evangelism in the 90's*

RadhakrishnanPillai and D. Sivanandhan – *Chanakyas's 7 Secrets of Leadership*

Reji Samuel – *Accountability in Leadership* – Paper presents at AALP, 2014

Rick Farlely – *Attitudes of Great Leaders*

Richard J. Kreir – *Understanding and developing Christian Accountability* (article)

Richard J. Goossen and R. Paul Stevens – *Entrepreneurial Leadership* – *Finding you calling, Making Difference*

R.M. Lala – *In Search of Ethical Leadership*

Robin Sharma – *Leadership Wisdom*

Robert Donald – *Characteristics of Christian Leadership* – Paper presented at AALP, 2014

Robert Bacal – *The role of the Facilitator* – Understanding what facilitators really do!

Robert Figureroa, *Leadership in Joshua*, Inspired Christian.org

Spears L. – *Reflections on leadership*

Tamyra Freeman – *Servant – Leader as Creative Problem Solving*

Titre Ande – *A Guide to Leadership*

Timothy Z. Witmer – *The Shepherd Leader*

Viv Thomas – *Future Leader*

Water V Wright – *Relationship Leadership* – A Biblical Model for Leadership Service Christian Leadership.net

www.meaningfulllife.com

www.MinTool.com – quipping for Ministry

www.leadershipletter.com – Abusive Leaders

www.intothyword.org

www.Gladiators for God

www.leadership – with – you.com

www.gotquestions.com

www.pinnetreeweb.com

www.churchleadership.org

www. biblical – inspiration. org

www.leadershippletters.com

www.findinggtruthmatters.org

Growing in the knowledge of Jesus, Bible Study Christ www.executableeoutlines.com

Leadership Based on Biblical Principles – Leadership from King Solomon

The Word in Life, Study Bible. New King James Version, Nelson

ecoggins.hubpages.com